Renaissance

The fall and rise of a king

MARLA SKIDMORE

First published in Great Britain as a softback original in 2018

Copyright © Marla Skidmore

The moral right of this author has been asserted.

Typeset in Adobe Garamond Pro

Editing, design, typesetting and publishing by UK Book Publishing

www.ukbookpublishing.com

ISBN: 978-1-912183-29-6

'Good name in man and woman...

Is the immediate jewel of their souls;

...he that filches from me my good name

...makes me poor indeed.'

(Othello III.iii.155-62)

Author's Note

This story is inspired by the discovery of Richard III's remains on 25th August 2012 and my own firm and long held belief that he was not the monstrous villain of the Tudor Histories and Shakespeare's play. I have always preferred to view him in the same light as his great biographer Paul Murray Kendal, who wrote: 'He was thirty-two years old, had reigned two years, one month, twenty-eight days. The only language, it turned out, in which he had been able to communicate himself successfully to the world was the terse idiom of courage, and the chief subject he had been given to express was violence. It had begun for him as a child in violence and it had ended in violence; the brief span between had been a tale of action and hard service with small joy and much affliction of spirit. If he had committed a grievous wrong he had sought earnestly to do great good. And through his darkening days he had kept to the end a golden touch of magnanimity. Men do not forget how the last of the Plantagenets had died. Polydore Vergil, Henry Tudor's official historian, felt compelled to record king Richard, alone, was killed fighting manfully in the thickest press of his enemies.'

My tale is an amalgamation of historical facts, contemporary events and my own imagination. The names of most of the characters will be familiar to those interested in English history; in their development and the motivation behind their actions I have brought my own interpretations into play but they are, I hope, backed by plausibility. I have endeavoured to remain true to historical fact and wherever possible I have tried not to distort time and place.

In conclusion I want to thank all those who have helped me during the last eighteen months – my husband Lt Col (Retd) Alan Skidmore for his military insights, his patience during my frequent crises of confidence and for taking over the running of our household whilst I, as he put it, 'wrestled with Richard'; my good friend Cris Connor for keeping me on the straight and narrow with regard to Richard III's world and the battle of Bosworth; to Janet Ratcliffe for her objective comments on the first draft; my sister Anita Chapman for her long suffering listening; and my fellow writers in 'Chapter and Verse' for their unfailing support.

M.S.

Marton-le-Moor, January 2017

When the killing blow struck from behind, his mauled and savaged body welcomed it gladly and his weary, grieving soul gratefully embraced the hereafter.

Chapter 1

The morning of 22nd August 1485

The plain of Redemore in Leicestershire

Nothing was turning out the way he envisaged. The rebels had not buckled under the arrow storm he'd unleashed nor did they break beneath the pounding of his heavy artillery. That wily fox Oxford then surprised him with an attack on his vanguard's flank. He sent in reinforcements with orders for Norfolk to fall back, form a crescent around the enemy wedge and then gore both sides driving them inward. The tactic worked. Oxford's assault lost momentum and began to crumble but the shrilling of 'retire to the standards' by the rebel trumpets and the enemy's suddenly rapid disengagement and retreat towards their banners in response, snatched away the advantage they had gained. Above the tumult of the battle their captains could be heard repeatedly roaring out the command to "keep close order... stay within ten paces of your standard...do not pursue the foe!". Frustrated and perplexed by this strange behaviour and fearing a trap, Norfolk held back his troops until the fierce battle call of the Plantagenets rang out over the field. Then he hurled them at the enemy with even greater ferocity.

Richard swallowed hard; an expression of raw grief passed over his stony features. As always, his old friend had put himself in the thickest press of the fighting; this time his courage and loyalty had cost him his life. The troops faltered when news of their commander's death spread through the ranks but they rallied when Surrey ably stepped into his father's shoes. For hours now his army had been locked in vicious hand-to-hand combat with Henry Tudor's mercenaries and were making little headway against them. Exhaustion was taking its toll. Discipline was breaking down. Men were beginning to slink away. Richard's flint hard gaze scanned the enemy's dispositions, looking for any opportunity to end the bloody deadlock. A flurry of activity far behind the rebel lines caught his attention. Narrowing his eyes against the bright morning sun he strained to see through the swirling dust of combat. There on horseback at the top of a small rise next to his red-dragon standard was the figure of Henry Tudor. He was on the move. Until now he had resolutely kept to the rear – well out of danger; content to let the Earl of Oxford do his fighting for him. Surrounding him were his personal guard and a large company of mounted reserve troops and bringing up the rear was the unit of pikemen that Francis and his scouting patrols had warned him of. They were there to form a bristling protective hedge around the Tudor to ensure his escape should the royal army get too close. Richard's keen soldier's eyes travelled over them. Something about them seemed not quite right. He pushed his mount forward the better to see and scrutinized them carefully. Their formation was sloppy and unregimented, their long lethal steel-tipped poles were laid carelessly back over their shoulders. These men showed none of the sharply drilled discipline of the famed, fearsome Swiss pikemen that he was expecting to see; which armies all over Europe dreaded facing. They were French infantry and finding themselves so far in the rebel rear, they evidently felt safe enough to completely let down their guard.

Richard's lips curled as he watched the Tudor and his party carefully begin skirting the marsh – his local guides had clearly made him aware of the risk that it still posed. A scorching August sun had shone down on the plain for days, baking the boggy ground rock-hard, but beneath its rutted and crusted surface a network of tiny rills still ran ready to snare the unwary. He knew exactly where Henry Tudor was heading. The traitor, who had bargained away English rights to the French crown and promised to hand back England's French territories in return for money and troops, was on his way to grovel to the Stanley brothers. The duplicitous pair were running true to form, staying aloof from the battle so they could be sure of being on the winning side. A fierce anger rose in him, his calloused fingers clenched involuntarily on the reins of his war horse. White Syrie's head tossed in annoyance; the Courser's hooves stamped on the ground as the bit was pulled sharply against its soft mouth. Reaching down to soothe his restive mount, Richard's gaze sharpened as he followed the Earl of Richmond's progress. In his desperation to reach Lord Thomas and his brother, Sir William, Henry Tudor was unwittingly making himself a target. Richard's heart began to hammer against his ribs – here was the chance he was looking for! He could take the battle to the Tudor himself and finish this bloodshed with one swift stroke. The risk was enormous. Speed and the element of surprise were crucial. If he was to have a chance of succeeding, he had to catch Henry Tudor and his bodyguards completely unawares. It meant riding directly across William Stanley's front and getting to him before the rebels could rally and Stanley could intervene. And if fortune favoured him, as they scrambled to take their positions, gaps would be left in the pikemen's defensive barrier and their long unwieldy poles would not be completely in place, before he and his knights reached them. An icy calm descended upon him. Resolution stamped itself upon his stern features. He would throw his destiny into the hands of Fate! Every muscle in his lean frame tightened in readiness for action.

He leant forward and stretched out a heavily mailed arm to Sir Richard Ratcliffe. "My lance if you please, sir." His friend, who insisted upon riding into this battle beside him as his esquire of the body, thrust the long iron-tipped spear into his waiting fist. Straightening up, Richard turned to face the rest of his household knights. The small faithful band of battle-hardened friends and followers, his constant companions for many years, were mounted, armoured and ready for action. Richard looked each of them in the eye; grave and composed they gazed silently back at him. They did not need to be told his intention. The tactic was bold and desperate, in all likelihood many of them would die in its execution, but none of them flinched from what he asked of them. Their loyalty to this man was absolute. They would not fail him and were prepared to follow him into Hell itself if he led them there. Richard lifted himself up in his stirrups so that all might hear him. "We ride to take Henry Tudor." He paused and gazed unseeingly into the distance, then in a strong and determined voice he vowed, "I will make an end… either of war or of life… will die as king or win victory on this field!"

Turning, he raised a gauntleted arm and signalled to his trumpeters. Once again, the battle call of the fearsome Plantagenets rang out over the plain. Then raising his lance high into the air, he pointed his weapon forward to advance. His horse moved forward at a walk. With those he most trusted riding close beside and behind him, the king skirted the northern flank of the royal army. As they gathered speed a sudden gust of wind unfurled the banners above their heads. In the morning breeze Richard's white boar and the royal lions and lilies streamed out over the battlefield, clearly visible to the rebel mercenaries. Transfixed with astonishment and disbelief at what they were seeing, no one moved to intercept them. With his quarry in his sights, Richard urged his horse to a canter. As they swept past the stationary cavalry of Sir William Stanley towards the dragon banner of Cadwallader, he caught a glimpse of rank upon rank of mounted men in bright red jackets. Richard shouted the order to charge and slammed his visor down. His men rowelled their horses to a full gallop. A voice from amongst Stanley's cavalry swore loudly, "God's wounds! They are mad!"

"Aye but 'tis a magnificent madness," responded an admiring voice. Alerted by the swelling thunder of horses' hooves, Henry Tudor and his men halted in puzzlement. They froze horror-struck when they turned to see the king at the head of a company of heavily armoured knights bearing down on them at tremendous speed. The dawning realization that they were under attack galvanized the Tudor's bodyguards into action but confusion and terror slowed their responses.

The clamour of the battle faded as Richard and White Syrie raced towards the milling mass of infantry and horsemen. As he drew nearer he heard the desperate screaming of orders. Through the narrow slit of his sights he saw riders forcing their rearing horses into line and the steel ranks of the Pretender's pike-guard rush forward and begin to close around him. A gap briefly appeared, and through it spurring his horse straight towards him, charged a giant of a man on a massive destrier. He knew from the man's size that it could only be Sir John Cheyne. The man who had once been his brother Edward's personal champion, who had patiently taught his younger self the skills of mounted combat and how to get the better of a larger and heavier opponent, was upon him before Richard could wheel his mount around. A touch from Cheyne's spurs had his horse lunging forward. They crashed together. Cheyne bellowed his challenge and raised his arm to make the killing blow with his enormous battle-axe but fury gave Richard almost superhuman strength. Pulling sharply back on his reins, he raked his spurs along White Syrie's flanks; the horse screamed and reared. Richard thrust downwards with his lance; Sir John reeled then toppled from the saddle. Trumpets blared frantically. He found himself under attack from all sides. Oblivious to the blows that rained down on him and the screams of horses and dying men, he dropped his lance and began to swing his own gleaming axe with deadly precision. Francis Lovell, Robert Percy and the Stafford brothers surged forward. Surrounding him in a tight protective ring, they slashed their way onward thrusting their horses and their bodies in front of him, forging a way through the Tudor's bodyguards. The swirling dust cleared, and for a brief moment beyond the heaving mass, Richard caught a glimpse of his enemy. He spurred his mount forward and then he was there. Only a few paces away, attempting to conceal himself behind his French pikemen was the Pretender. Elation rushed through Richard giving man and horse the impetus to crash through the pikemen's partially formed barrier. Behind it, ashen faced and trembling, the man who would be king made little effort to defend himself. Henry Tudor fumbled for a moment at his scabbard, then, letting his hand drop limply to his side, he waited for the king to strike. Sir William Brandon, the Tudor's standard bearer, flung himself between Richard and his prey. Swinging his battle-axe up in a high glittering arc, Richard brought it down with brutal force. Down went the red dragon banner and William Brandon lay dead on the trampled ground. He drew his sword; at last he had had the treasonous cur at his mercy. The euphoria of victory sizzled through his veins as he held at sword point the man who would steal his crown. His gamble had paid off – he had won the day! The Tudor whelp would learn what it meant to rebel against his king. He would pay the ultimate price for his overweening ambition and Lancastrian aspirations to rule England would be vanquished once and for all. "Take him!" He pulled his mount back to allow Francis Lovell and the others who had ridden beside him to surround his prisoner, but before anyone could move, hordes of Stanley cavalry smashed into their flank and rear. Richard and his small company of knights swung round and found themselves facing the onslaught of a vast army of hostile Welshmen. Seeing Richard separate himself from the main body of his army, the Stanley brothers had seized their opportunity for treachery. Richard looked across the battlefield towards the silver lion banner of Norfolk, and to his despair he saw it waver then become engulfed by swarms of French and Scottish troops. His trumpets rang out the urgent call to retreat. A harsh bitter sound escaped the king's throat when he looked towards where his rear-guard should now be. There was little point in signalling for aid; Northumberland had not moved into position. All along, at the back of his mind, Richard had questioned whether Henry Percy would actually fight. His tardy arrival the night before should have warned Richard not to rely on him.

Incandescent with fury at having victory snatched away, Richard lost all sense of self-preservation. With the desire for vengeance and blood running hot in his veins, he swung his mount around and with a guttural roar of "treason!" he spurred his mount forward and charged straight towards the despicable turncoats who had betrayed him. When the red mist of rage cleared from his brain he saw himself surrounded. Relentlessly his enemies drove him deeper and deeper into the marsh where the crusted ground crumbled away beneath White Syrie's hooves and brought him to his knees. Unhorsed, Richard kept the slavering Lancastrian hounds at bay with the skill of his sword, but his weary brain acknowledged the stark reality that they would soon close in for the kill. Beneath his armour his chest and one side of his body were coated with blood from a deep wound underneath his arm that was sapping away his strength; he could not hold them off for much longer. *'I will not be taken alive! Better a quick, honourable death than being taken prisoner – humiliated and dependent upon the mercy of rebels and traitors!'*

Grimly resolved he fought on. He was no longer feeling the blows from the dozens of weapons that smashed through his armour, when the halberd crashed viciously into the back of his skull and sent white hot pain radiating down his spine. As he spiralled into dark nothingness brief random thoughts flashed through his mind... *'this is what it feels like to die... Norfolk was right... the circlet around my helmet was a magnet for every glory-seeking Lancastrian bastard on this field... Anne!... be waiting for me, sweeting...I am coming.'*

Chapter 2

Light filtered through Richard's closed eyelids; his eyes slowly opened. They remained unfocused and dazed for a few moments but quickly regained their sharp clarity as the fog of unconsciousness cleared from his brain. He inhaled deeply then coughed as his lungs were assaulted by the acrid stench of gunpowder, over-ridden horses, blood and sweat. He was lying on the battlefield. He gasped in disbelief; against all odds he was still alive! Vivid images of those final moments before his enemies overwhelmed him, crowded into his mind. He was down on one knee, one hand braced on the ground, the other gripping the hilt of his sword, using it as a prop to keep himself upright. He was surrounded by Welsh soldiers. They prowled around him – nostrils flaring, bodies tense, sword, mace and pike at the ready; circling him like a pack of feral dogs. He tried to struggle to his feet but his legs gave way and he sank to his knees once more. The halberd slammed into the back of his head with such savage force that the whole of his compact frame jerked forward convulsively; his spine arching with the impact, then his body folded forward and slid to the ground. Richard's belly heaved, bile rose in his throat making him swallow rapidly. That had surely been the moment of his death! No man could survive such a blow and he had already been badly wounded even before the halberd smashed into his skull. He could still feel the burning pain of the sword thrust deep into his side and the agony of splintering bone and tearing muscle when the halberd felled him. He was utterly confounded to find himself alive! He lay still and took stock. Amazingly he could find no sign of injury nor could he detect the stickiness of congealed blood anywhere. There was no pain, only the dull familiar ache of over-taxed muscles tested in combat. He was breathing easily; he could move all his limbs. Richard's strongly marked brows drew together in a deep frown – *'I should be dead!'* His bewildered brain raced, searching for answers but found none. A deep sense of misgiving crept over him, and along with it came the uneasy feeling of being watched. Slowly and carefully he lifted his head; there was nothing to see. On one side, dappled sunlight frolicked through the foliage of a copse of slender saplings, on the other there was rough pasture. Beyond that he could see ripe ears of corn blowing in the wind. 'I was mortally wounded! *Why am I not dead?'* The question kept running through his mind until his head ached with the effort of trying to find an explanation for his miraculous survival. Richard lay back and let the springy marsh grass pillow his tired body. Raising a shaky forearm to shield his eyes from the sun's glare, he lay back and endeavoured to calm his tumultuous thoughts. As he listened to the steady rhythmic beat of his heart the thought slipped into his head that perhaps it was simply that his Creator had decided that he would not die on the plain of Redemore today; that treachery and betrayal

11

had not been allowed to prosper entirely. Slowly the feelings of apprehension and trepidation holding his body in their tight grip began to ease. He told himself to stop being a fool. The Almighty had seen fit to preserve him – instead of being fearful and suspicious, he should be on his knees giving thanks.

He raised himself up on one elbow and saw that he was lying on the slope of a small hillock, shielded from the sun by a dense thicket of willow and alder. Above him, high in the hot August sky, black crows circled slowly, readying themselves to dive and feed on the dead and dying – '*how he hated those filthy scavengers!*' Battle-hardened veteran that he was, the scene of slaughter and butchery that met his eyes in the field below still made him retch. Amongst dead horses, broken carts and abandoned weapons, half hidden by long tufts of marsh grass, lay the bodies of the dead and wounded of both armies. Their limbs twisted grotesquely, they were strewn across the rough pasture, the sun's rays glinting off their swords and breastplates. It was as if some giant evil puppet master, grown tired of his playthings, had wantonly destroyed them and then flung them away. A light breeze ruffled the long green fronds causing them to swirl and drift over the mangled and mutilated bodies; as if a disapproving Nature was attempting to spread a concealing veil over the bloody spectacle. A pall of smoke still hanging over the silent field was starting to thin, beginning a slow writhing climb up into the cloudless sky. In the distance, on the edge of the plain, the red dragon standard of Henry Tudor, and the red rose banner of Lancaster fluttered victoriously in the warm summer air.

As he fought to control the gorge rising in his throat the thought struck Richard that, having seen him go down, his supporters would surely think their king dead and their cause lost. From the position of the sun in the sky he calculated that it was now well after noon. They would either have fled the battlefield or surrendered. Richard felt he ought to be filled with despair and fear for what the future held but all he could feel at this moment was a profound sense of gratitude at having eluded death, although the ugly reality of his predicament swiftly began to filter into his mind. Any moment now Henry Tudor and his treacherous supporters would come looking for his body. To claim Richard's throne the Tudor needed to prove that he was dead. The people had to see his corpse; when it could not be found and there was a possibility that he was still alive, there would be a hue and cry. He was about to become a hunted fugitive! His mind began to race. He chastised himself. *'Don't lie there wasting precious time, Dickon my lad, it could cost you your life! Give thanks to your Creator for preserving you to fight another day and get on your feet! Get off this battlefield now!'* He took a moment to think about what he should do next. *'Disguise yourself, make your way north,'* he told himself. *'The people of the North have always been loyal to you. You are Richard, their Lord of the North. Once you are amongst your people again you can regroup and take back your kingdom.'*

Richard paused for a long anguished moment when he recalled that he was alone now; the weight of recent grief and loss lay heavily in his heart. His brothers were all dead. Edward, his son, was buried at Middleham and he had laid his beloved Anne to rest in the Abbey at Westminster only a few short months ago. An insidious little voice inside his head asked... *'is it worth all the struggle and bloodshed? Would it not be easier to leave England –*

seek sanctuary with my sister Margaret in Burgundy and live there in comfortable obscurity? Why not let Henry Tudor have the throne with all its turmoil, rumour and rebellion?' Then he heard his father's voice growling out the rule that he insisted all his sons live by, *"A Plantagenet never gives up...the throne of England is ours by right!"*

Pushing aside destructive self-doubt, Richard raised himself to his knees. A feeling of light-headedness made him sit back on his haunches, and as he allowed his swirling senses to settle, it slowly dawned on him that he had managed this manoeuvre effortlessly. There was no armour weighing him down and restricting his movements. Frowning, he rose stiffly to his feet and looked down – whilst he had been unconscious someone had removed his armour. He was dressed only in his quilted gambeson, leggings and soft leather boots. In confusion he looked around. *Were the human vultures that scavenged the fields of death already engaged in their grisly task of robbing the dead and wounded? If so, when they saw him still breathing, why hadn't they killed and stripped him?* Raising his left hand, he saw that he was still wearing the heavy gold ring, engraved with his boar device and personal vow to his wife, 'A Vous Me Ly' – given to him by Anne on the anniversary of their first year of marriage.

With every instinct sharpened and on the alert for danger, Richard's gaze swept over the battlefield. Nothing moved. The eerie silence, disturbed only by the buzzing of clouds of black flies hovering over the bloody corpses, unsettled him. Anxiety began to bubble up inside him again. He hated this feeling of not being totally in control. Cursing softly beneath his breath he rubbed the back of his neck and tried to ease the tension building there. After a moment he took a long shuddering breath to calm his whirling thoughts and let the pragmatist in him take over. *'Don't fret about questions you cannot answer – it's a dangerous waste of time! Use your wits, Dickon. Think! What would you do in The Tudor's place when no dead king's body can be found?'* He gave an ironic chuckle – that's easily answered. *'Immediately send out search parties to scour the countryside and every town and village within a day's march from here; station lookouts on every road north...'* And so his own plan of action began to take shape. *He would stay off the well-trodden routes to the North, using Drovers' tracks he would first head east – deep into the Lincolnshire Wolds, only then would he turn northward – towards the Humber. Once he was across that great river he would be safe in the loyal North. He would make his way to York and there in that trusty city, he would rally his supporters.*

Richard weighed up the practicalities of his plan. Travelling alone and on foot through the wild, densely wooded countryside of Middle England and the North was a dangerous undertaking. He would be seen as an easy target for those cutthroats and thieves who preyed on lone unprotected travellers. He had to equip himself for his journey. He required a weapon with which to defend himself, and also any small items that he could barter or sell for food. There was no alternative but to take what he needed from the dead lying in the field below. His ring was useless: its obvious quality and the boar engraving would swiftly raise suspicions. Reluctantly, Richard began to make his way down the slope. The muscles in his jaw grew rigid; his throat thickened with shame and self-loathing at what he was about to do. *'I'm joining the ranks of those filthy scavengers, who prey on the fallen,'* he thought in disgust. Taking a deep breath, hands fisting against the compulsion to turn and flee, he forced himself forward towards a tangled mound of bodies. Desperate hand-to-hand fighting had taken place here. The soft ground beneath them was churned up and stained deep rusty ochre with their blood. The air was heavy with the stench of brutal butchery. Swallowing the sour tang in his mouth, Richard resolutely crouched down. Reaching towards the nearest body he found himself gazing into the stiff dead face of one of his own personal guard. Flinching, Richard drew back and straightened up. He looked more closely at the other dead men lying at his feet. His teeth clenched, as he fought to hold back an overwhelming wave of sadness when he identified at least half a dozen of his closest knight companions; men who had fought with him at Barnet, Tewkesbury and in the Scottish campaign. They lay together in a tight semi-circle, and in their midst, stained with their blood but still protected by the hacked and butchered body of Sir Percy Thirlwall, his standard bearer, lay his own red and blue banner bearing the white rose and white boar. His loyal and courageous comrades-in-arms had ridden into the melee after their reckless king in an effort to protect him, and had been cut down trying to do so. With intense sorrow and deep remorse washing through him, Richard knelt and bowed his head in prayer. *'I beg forgiveness, my brave and gentle friends, my reckless foolhardiness cost you your lives.'* He swallowed hard and wondered again why he was still alive. Then with trembling fingers he reached forward to close, what seemed to him, the reproachful eyes of the nearest fallen knight.

Raised voices from behind the crest of the hill had him lifting his head abruptly. He listened intently. "He's somewhere hereabouts, Sire. I'm sure of it! I remember that small hillock and that stand of trees. Somewhere just below we had King Rich...I mean the usurper surrounded," an agitated voice confirmed then rambled on excitedly, "...'twasn't easy to bring 'im down...fought something fierce he did...gave a good account of 'iself...gutted a few of us well and good 'afore the halberd finally dispatched 'im."

"Then find the body without further delay. I need proof to show the people so there will be no rumours of his survival to stoke up rebellions," a thin, impatient voice ordered.

"Christ's wounds!" Richard swore under his breath; he had run out of time. Henry Tudor was already here on the battlefield searching for him. Arming himself with a fallen knight's sword, he swiftly pounded up the rise, throwing himself behind the dense foliage of the small copse of trees.

Concealed behind a trailing curtain of willow branches, Richard watched as Henry Tudor's men spread out and methodically began to search for his body. The rebels showed scant respect for the dead. Bodies were turned over and examined, anything of value found on them was plundered and then they were roughly dragged to one side to form a steadily mounting pile of corpses. Any of Richard's men found to be still alive were dispatched with a swift and merciless efficiency, as the occasional choking gasp and abruptly cut-off moan bore witness to. It was only a matter of time before his enemies worked their way up the hill. Resolutely his fingers tightened on the hilt of his borrowed sword. He would not cower here waiting to be found; nor would he allow himself to be taken alive to face an ignominious death at the hands of a man whose claim to the throne was so dubious, that it was a travesty – through a female and tainted by illegitimacy. Richard closed his eyes. *'Better to die fighting.'* Taking a deep breath he moved out from beneath the trees. A shout of triumph halted him before he could step into the open. "Here he is! This is 'im – this is Richard! We've found the king!" Surprise held him immobile. His gaze swung over to the place where his dead comrades lay, to see two red-coated Welshmen bending over the mangled body of Sir Percy.

Alerted by their cry of recognition, the lanky figure of Henry Tudor strode rapidly across the field towards them, trailed by his uncle, Jasper Tudor, and the Commander of his army, the Earl of Oxford. "Show me," he demanded, his small, light blue eyes narrowing in anticipation. When they failed to move quickly enough, he roughly pushed aside the two excited soldiers and pulled away the bloody banner shrouding the body himself. Richard smiled cynically. *'You are about to be disappointed, you treacherous bastard, I'm still very much alive.'* Henry's narrow-shouldered, slightly stooping figure took on an uncanny stillness as he stared intently down at the body lying at his feet; his thin, sallow face showed no emotion. After long silent moments he raised his eyes heavenward. Inhaling deeply, he smiled. "It is done. England is mine," he whispered beneath his breath. Then giving his men a curt nod of acknowledgment, he pointed to a grimy, undernourished grey cob placidly cropping the grass a short distance below Richard's hiding place. "Strip the body and load it on to the horse," Henry ordered. The men eagerly sprang to do his bidding. Hearing Henry Tudor's instructions, Richard flinched; his lips curled contemptuously at his enemy's lack of knightly chivalry and respect for a fallen adversary. Recollection of Henry's odd instruction, however, rapidly turned his disgust to bemusement. *'Is the whoreson intending to pass Sir Percy off as me?'* Richard wondered, shaking his head in disbelief. *'He cannot be so lack-witted. Sir Percy was a very large and robustly built man, I am of a much slighter stature.'* Mystified, Richard watched and waited as the two men struggled to untangle Sir Percy's heavy body *from the corpses of the other dead knights.*

Word quickly spread that the slain king had been found. Searchers all over the battlefield abandoned their grisly work. Jubilant Lancastrians of every rank from humble foot soldier to high ranking knights gathered round the spot where the supposed body of the dead king lay; craning their necks and jostling one another to get a better look at the royal corpse. Suddenly a hush descended upon the assembled soldiers. Richard inhaled sharply when he got a glimpse of the naked, battered body being dragged by its feet through the silently parted men – it was not the corpse of his standard bearer. A low rumble of protest began to ripple through the men. "For shame! Is there a need to dishonour him so? He was an anointed king. He fought bravely," muttered a rough voice filled with a soldier's respect for a fallen adversary. Henry Tudor's body tensed at the criticism, his narrow lips flattened in anger. Drawing himself up to his full height, he swung round. "Who dares to question the actions of his king?" he snarled, glaring at them; his stony stare challenging anyone to say anything further. Fury sizzled along Richard's veins. He was unable to hold back a cynical bark of laughter. *'The treacherous cur had yet to be accepted by his peers and Parliament, and be properly anointed and crowned, yet already he styled himself king.'*

The elevation of the ground and the protection of the trees

gave Richard a clearer view of the body that had been roughly dropped on to the soft grass beside the hooves of the waiting horse. This man's frame was slight, yet even in death, the tough sinew and corded muscles of a hardened warrior were evident. Richard felt a strange sense of recognition. *Did he know this man?* He felt compelled to take a closer look and edged further down the slope, to the fringe of the trees – as far as he could go without being seen. The feeling of familiarity intensified. He strained forward, narrowing his eyes to study the dead man more closely.

He was bloody, so very, very bloody; his shoulders, chest and back were coated in it and his thick, dark blonde hair was matted and caked with it. There was a deep gash in his side from a sword thrust between the ribs. The back of the poor wretch's skull had been crushed and there was a jagged gaping wound between his shoulder and neck. Richard's body stilled; a feeling of foreboding crept through him. His scalp began to prickle, the hair at the back of his neck lifted. The injuries he was staring down at were agonisingly familiar. Chills skittered up his spine. His heart started pounding. *'Enough of this foolishness!'* he rebuked himself sternly. *'Hundreds of men received such wounds in the battle.'* Slowly Richard let out the breath he had unknowingly been holding. Shaking his head, he scolded himself soundly once more for allowing irrational imaginings to get the better of him. Then his eyes took in the twist in the dead man's spine. Richard froze, his eyes widened in disbelief. *'Very few in his Court even remembered his weakness... it only troubled him when he had been on a horse for too long – then his back stiffened and his legs ached...'* A cold sweat sprang out all over his body. He began to shake uncontrollably. *'No!'* His mind screamed a denial. The naked body lying on the trampled grass below was not his own corpse! *'It cannot be so! I live!'* Richard's vision blurred, the world began to spin around him. The sword he was holding slipped from his suddenly slack grip. Making the sign of the cross, he stumbled backwards until his calves hit the moss-covered trunk of a rotting tree. He slumped down, dropping his head, which felt as if it was about to explode, into cold clammy hands. Unable to stop himself, he raised fearful eyes once more to the horror confronting him. Transfixed, he watched as the dead man was carelessly slung over the back of the waiting horse; his feet hanging down one side, his head and arms on the other. To secure him in place a rope was tied around his neck, passed beneath the animal's belly and attached to his feet. The soft gleam of gold on the third finger of one hand caught Richard's eye. Breathing suddenly became difficult, his breath rasped in his throat as he gasped for air. Questions scurried round his fevered brain like rats caught in a trap. *If that was his corpse and he was dead, why was he still here on the battlefield? He had made his confession and been absolved of his sins before going into battle; why had he not joined his Creator in the next world? Was he a ghost – doomed to haunt this battlefield for eternity? If he was a ghost, why did he still have all his senses – he could see, hear, touch, smell, and feel?*

The muscles in Richard's stomach grew rigid as he fought to control the primal scream of terror rising in his throat. Jerkily he stood up and ran shaking hands down his tense body. His trembling fingers reached up to touch his mouth, his nose, his eyes; they ran over his brow, through his hair, drawing it back from his face to knead the knotted muscles at the back of his neck. *'If I am dead why do I feel so alive?'* The question spun round and round in his mind in a never-ending cycle. Finally, in a desperate attempt to convince himself that he was still amongst the living, Richard picked up the sword he had dropped. He stared intently at it then slowly and deliberately he drew the razor sharp blade across the open palm of his hand, pressing it deep. The burning pain made the breath hiss through his clenched teeth, but seeing no hot rush of blood run from the gaping wound he fell despairingly to his knees, clutching the injured hand to his chest.

Chapter 3

"Do no further harm to yourself my son, 'tis a sin," a deep authoritative voice from behind, accompanied by the firm pressure of strong fingers on his shoulder, made Richard start. Fear shot through him. Flinging up a protective arm, he swung round to find himself looking into the craggy face of a tall, robustly-built monk wearing the coarse habit of the Franciscan order. Translucent, icy blue eyes frowned down at him in disapproval. "Cease this futile struggle against the truth and stop torturing yourself!" Giving him no time to move or speak, the monk pulled him to his feet and turned him to face the battlefield. "You must accept that this day you died on that field." Suddenly weak Richard's legs gave way. He would have fallen if the monk's brawny arms had not held him upright. "You've never lacked courage, Richard Plantagenet," the monk's gravelly voice growled into his ear. "Go!" His powerful hands eased their hard grip. "Test the truth of my words. Your enemies cannot see you. You need take but a few short steps to examine the mauled and brutalized shell that was once a king, lying on the back of that horse." Still held in the monk's supporting hold, Richard hesitated. Bleakly he gazed out over the battlefield whilst his tortured brain struggled vainly against the reality of his death but in truth he could no longer deny it. The gruesome bloody proof was right there below him, slung over the back of a worn-out nag. Closing his eyes, Richard gave a long painful sigh of acceptance.

The injustice of his fate began to burn like alchemists' acid through Richard's veins. His defeat and death through treachery and betrayal; the ascendancy of a man he deeply despised to the throne of his ancestors, was a physical torment almost beyond bearing. It felt as if a dagger was being thrust and twisted deeply into his gut. He doubled over with the pain of it and clamped his teeth to contain the bitter curses of rage and recrimination that he wanted to hurl up to the heavens. *'Why?'* His mind screamed the question at his god. *'Why have you allowed this to happen? I tried to rule justly and with honour for the good of the whole realm, for commoner and great noble alike.'* His chest heaved and his fists clenched as he fought for control. Finally, having regained command over himself, Richard straightened and stepped away from the monk, regarding him with wary distrustful eyes. "Then tell me, Sir Monk," he rasped, forcing the words through a mouth made dry with dread by thoughts of what now awaited him, "why my body still moves, and speaks?" He pulled an overhanging willow branch towards him and rubbed the delicate surface of a long slender frond between his finger and thumb… "enjoys touch?" He frowned down at the deep gash in his palm and then abruptly thrust the injured hand towards the monk… "feels pain?"

Compassion softened the monk's rough-hewn features. He

had been forced to stand by and watch as the young king met his death. The souls of those violently ripped from their living bodies were always the hardest to convince and the manner of his death had indeed been brutally savage. Seeing the bewilderment and dread behind Richard's eyes, Father Gilbert tried to give him an explanation that he would understand. "Because you now exist in another sphere..." The look of utter incomprehension on the king's face stopped him. He tried again, "Until your soul is accepted into the next world you will exist here – in a space that is somewhere between heaven and earth. You will experience all the physical pains and emotions of the living and your five senses will remain with you until your soul has been tried and deemed fit to join the Creator but the blood of life will no longer flow in your veins. I, Father Gilbert, am to be your guide, I will help you make the transition."

Richard's eyes narrowed in hostile suspicion; his sharp agile mind immediately pounced on the monk's words. "My guide? What need have I of a guide?" he snapped. "I confessed and received absolution before the battle. If I died–" his brain still denied the reality of it– "then I died in a state of grace and should instantly have taken my place in heaven. What proof have I that you are not the Devil's emissary sent to lure me into his fiery world of torture and torment?" Hearing Father Gilbert's rich belly laugh in response, Richard grew rigid with anger. "Do not mock me, monk – if that is what you truly are," he snarled.

The web of lines around the monk's eyes crinkled in amusement. "Look carefully at me, my young Doubting Thomas. Find the proof for yourself." Richard's gaze swept assessingly up and down the burly figure for a few moments, taking in the small silver crucifix hanging from a leather lace around Father Gilbert's neck and the larger wooden one dangling from the length of soft rope tied around his thick waist. His eyes widened in understanding. "Yes," the monk chuckled, "as you well know, neither Lucifer nor his minions can suffer our Lord's cross anywhere near them." Activity in the field below caught his attention and the humorous twinkle left his eyes; his face became solemn and set. He strode quickly to Richard's side, resting both his large hands firmly on the king's shoulders the monk steered him forward out of the trees. "Come, we can no longer linger here."

Chapter 4

"I care not how 'tis done but I wish every trace of him wiped out. There will be no grave, no burial rites and no tomb to become the rallying point for future Yorkist rebellions." Henry Tudor rapped out his orders, glaring balefully down at the naked corpse sprawled out on the rough wooden trestle in front of him. "And most surely there will be rebellions against me," Henry muttered to himself, "for he is too much admired and loved by the people of the North. The challenge to my right to rule this kingdom will come from there." Furthermore, Richard's courage in the face of a certain and terrible death was spreading rapidly throughout the city. Henry's own mercenaries were turning Richard's foolhardy cavalry charge into an act of heroic chivalry. Speculation was rife about Henry's own capture by the dead king and his failure to defend himself – *'saved and victorious only through Stanley treachery'* was being whispered behind shielded lips everywhere he went. The aura of a tragic, courageous legend was rapidly beginning to grow around Richard. Henry's victory was being overshadowed; his standing diminished before his grip on the throne was secure. This he would not allow! The men-at-arms guarding Richard's naked, despoiled body looked at each other in horror. One man, braver than his companions, stepped forward. "You would deny him a Christian burial, Sire?" he queried in a disbelieving voice. Henry slowly raised his head and stared at the guard who had dared to question him, the malice in his face had the man taking a hasty step backwards. "Toss him into the Soar so the fish can feed on his flesh or better yet take him into the forest where wolves and foxes can gorge on him and scatter his bones far and wide," he hissed. Turning on his heel, Henry strode rapidly down the nave of the Church of Our Lady of the Newarke. "See that it is done before the morrow." He flung his orders over his shoulder. "I want him gone!"

Father Gilbert watched Richard uneasily; his charge's rapid, shallow breathing and rigid posture told the monk that he was close to breaking. Looking back on the unhappy events of the day, he was astounded by Richard's grim stoicism in the face of the humiliations he had suffered as they followed in the wake of Henry Tudor's triumphant entry into Leicester – the city from which Richard had departed only two days ago entirely confident of victory, his banners flying proudly in the early morning breeze. Richard's spirit had been tested to its very limits. How much more could he bear?

They had emerged from the trees to see Henry's mercenaries forming a cavalcade with the horse bearing the royal corpse at the rear. Seeing so many enemy soldiers milling around, Richard immediately crouched into a defensive stance, bringing up his sword in readiness to fight off any attack. "Calm yourself," the monk soothed reassuringly, "pay heed to what I have told you. Remember – we do not occupy the same earthly space as the Living. They cannot see or hear us." As the monk finished speaking the order was given for the procession to move off the battlefield but before anyone could proceed, Henry Tudor's voice rapped out a sharp "hold!". Raking his spurs along his horse's flanks, he wheeled it round and spurred it along the long line of horses and men, coming to a rearing halt next to the nervous, sweating mount over whose bony back the dead king's body hung. He leant forward and pulled his heavy sword from its sheath, then with his sharp, sallow features twisting in hatred, Henry gave a vindictive snarl and drove it violently into the dead king's exposed buttock. In that moment Richard doubled over convulsively, then inhaling deeply he straightened. "Cowardly, dishonourable cur," he sneered contemptuously, "capable only of inflicting hurt upon the dead." The humiliation perpetrated upon his corpse burned agonisingly into Richard's soul.

As the triumphant Lancastrian procession passed through the village of Stoke Golding, shame and frustrated fury were heaped upon the humiliation Richard was already burdened with, by the arrival of the traitorous Sir William Stanley carrying the gold coronet Richard had worn into battle; somewhat battered but still recognisable as the royal crown. When Henry knelt and allowed himself to be crowned, a deep animal-like groan burst through Richard's tight lips. "It should not be so," his voice cracked with guilt and grief, "England's throne belongs to the House of Plantagenet and I have lost it. I am the cause of the end of Plantagenet rule over England!"

From that moment Richard was mute. For three days in silent torment, he watched as the citizens of Leicester came to gape at his naked body. And now in a final act of extreme malice, Henry had forbidden him a Christian burial; a right that belonged to the lowliest man and woman in the kingdom. Richard's tortured spirit could bear no more. He sank to the church floor. With his gaunt face pressed against the cold tiles and his arms stretched wide, Richard let out a guttural roar of agony. "Are my sins so great that I do not merit even the humblest of graves? Am I to be thrown away like kitchen waste?" he cried out in a tormented voice. Caught up in the depth of his despair, Richard failed to hear the heated, low-voiced discussion taking place between Henry's men-at-arms. They moved towards the trestle and looked down at his body; lines of pity were written on each tough face. The guard, who had challenged Henry, removed his long woollen cloak and carefully covered the dead king. "He was an anointed king, who courageously led his men into battle in defence of his throne; a warrior who fought bravely and died an honourable death. I will not be a party to such an unholy act," he muttered gruffly. With these words he turned on his heel, marched resolutely down the nave and left the church. Having nodded in silent agreement, the remaining guards positioned themselves protectively around the body.

Richard felt himself lifted to his feet. The monk stood beside him, a tall silent sentinel, watching over his charge who was digging deeply into his shattered and shredded soul for the courage to face the dishonourable disposal of his earthly remains. Long moments went by before Richard won the battle to regain his composure. Finally, he raised his head and in a voice laden with pain and despair, asked the questions that had been running through his brain since their arrival at the church. "Why? Why am I being tormented in this manner? I have accepted my death.

I need no further convincing. Are you showing me that I am damned for all eternity? Without a grave for my bones to rest in, where will my soul return to on the Day of Judgement?"

Father Gilbert stared wordlessly back at Richard; pity for the young king gnawed at his heart. He was sorely tempted into giving him the comfort of an explanation but he knew there could be no short cuts into the Afterlife; Richard had to pay all his dues. His expression tightened and he shook his head. "It is not yet time for you to know the answers to your questions," he answered enigmatically, guiding Richard firmly down the nave to the front entrance of the church. Its massive oak doors had been flung wide open, and in the churchyard beyond stood a rough farmer's cart. A couple of men-at-arms held it steady by its long wooden handles, another stood guard at its head. Richard recoiled in horror. "Sweet Jesu," he whispered hoarsely, "you intend for me to witness the carrying out of the Tudor's orders! I will not do it!" It took all Father Gilbert's considerable strength to restrain him as he struggled wildly to free himself and flee. "Be still, Richard Plantagenet! Look and listen," he ordered sternly.

With every muscle rigid in revulsion, Richard reluctantly stopped trying to free himself to see his body, cradled carefully in the arms of three robust Franciscan friars, being carried to the cart. Gently they laid him down on the slatted wooden floor and covered him with a friar's robe. Close behind walked the Abbot of Greyfriars monastery, accompanied by the guard who had hurried away from the church. "Be assured, sir, King Richard will be buried with all the rites of the Church. Masses will be said for the repose of his soul. His burial place, in front of the altar in the Choir of our church, is being prepared as we speak." Sighing sadly,

31

the Abbot reached out and stroked a gentle work-worn hand along Richard's covered body. "He looked with great favour upon our Order, always choosing his personal Chaplain from amongst the Franciscans." Deep in thought the Abbot gazed abstractedly into the distance, then gave another heartfelt sigh. "He was a just and good king who had a care for the common people," he continued in a low voice, "and will at least rest among those who love and honour him." Then more resolutely, the Abbot urged everyone into action. "We must make haste! The king must be laid safely in his grave this night, whilst the Earl of Richmond is still distracted by his victory celebrations." Then raising his voice slightly, the Abbot called all the men-at-arms to him. "Our thanks go to you all for alerting us to the Earl of Richmond's unkind intentions towards the king's mortal remains." Raising his hand he made the sign of the cross over their bowed heads. "God's blessings be upon you for your charity and care of a king's soul," he murmured in benediction. Satisfied with the rightness of their actions and unconcerned for the consequences should Henry discover that they had ignored his orders, the men-at-arms silently made their way out of the churchyard, dipping their heads in respect as they passed by the dead king. In the gathering dusk of a hot August evening, a sorrowful little procession of Franciscan friars began to wind its way through the dark narrow streets of Leicester, taking the king whom they loved to a simple, hastily dug grave in their monastery church. The last thing Richard heard as his strength drained away and merciful darkness claimed him was Father Gilbert murmuring, "Rest now, Richard Plantagenet, be at peace."

Chapter 5

Richard regained his senses to find himself lying, with his head resting on the monk's hard thighs, on a wide stone ledge cut into the roughly hewn walls of a cavernous nave-like space. He blinked. The vaulted ceiling and massive intricately-carved pillars reminded him of the great abbey church at Jervaulx, near his Middleham home, where he had often worshipped as a young boy. But here, no bright northern sunlight streamed through the leaded tracery of high arched windows, illuminating walls painted with scenes from the life of Our Lord and his Saints. Instead, the flickering flames from torches embedded in the stone high above his head, cast their dim light onto enormous iron-braced doors running along the length of both sides of the vast shadowy chamber, creating mysterious silhouettes on the empty stone flags at its centre. Without warning an intense feeling of homesickness swept through Richard, accompanied by a deep longing to just once more be able to roam across the Moors and Dales surrounding his beloved Yorkshire home. He closed his eyes and let pictures drift into his mind of that brief, happier time of his boyhood in the North shared with Francis and...*my*

Anne. He pressed the heel of his palm hard into his chest trying to ease the aching grief and the constricting bands of loneliness and desolation wrapped around his heart. He stirred restlessly; the pain of remembering was too much to bear. Venturing into the past was a futile and agonising exercise, so he gathered together his memories and returned them to the stone cell he had constructed around them in his mind; locking them once more behind its thick impenetrable walls. Having suppressed his unhappy reflections, he drew in a shaky breath and mentally shook himself; it was time to face whatever else was waiting to confront him in this harrowing, unknown universe in which he found himself.

His eyes snapped open to find Father Gilbert studying him, scrutinizing his face closely with narrowed, concerned eyes. "Well, monk, where have you brought me to now? What further torments have you devised for me?" he demanded roughly, trying to divert the monk's too-discerning gaze. Hearing the edge of sarcasm in Richard's voice, the monk's hard mouth lifted slightly in a small relieved smile; the young king's courage had reasserted itself. He was ready to face the next step. With mischief glinting in his eyes and a note of humour in his deep voice, Father Gilbert answered him. "Why, Richard, surely you have already guessed? You are in Purgatory."

Richard sat up abruptly and looked around; cocking his head he listened intently then gave the monk a long questioning look. *Where were the cries of pain and torment; the intense heat from the purifying fires?* His eyes flicked around the empty silent hall. *It was hard to believe that this was the place about which priests preached in such lurid detail; which most mortals went in abject terror of.* As if hearing his thoughts Father Gilbert nodded his head in solemn confirmation and in a more serious tone continued, "Purgatory, you will soon realise, is a condition of the mind and spirit as well as being a physical place." Seeing Richard's uncomprehending frown, the Monk explained: "Think about the experiences you have already undergone...what did you feel? Humiliation, shame, guilt, fear? Since the moment of your death, Richard Plantagenet, you have been in Purgatory – of the spirit and the senses, and now you are here in the physical place itself."

Richard shivered involuntarily as the realization struck home. *Holy God! He had in truth been consigned to Purgatory!* For long silent moments he sat and contemplated his fate. Then with a deep sigh he leant back against the cold stone wall behind him and rubbed his forehead abstractedly. *So much for his Confessor's assurances that he would immediately be transported to heaven should he be slain in the battle!'* He gave a humourless chuckle. Now that he was able to think clearly, he was somehow not really surprised at the monk's words. Ever since their strange meeting on the battlefield, a distant part of Richard's brain had recognised that the monk was guiding him through some sort of trial. Yet he could not resist challenging him – it was not in his nature to accept whatever he was told without question. "I confessed and received Absolution... died in a state of Grace... I even made provision in my Will for a Chantry Chapel to be built in the Minster at York and for priests to pray for the repose of my soul...the Church solemnly assures its people that if we are in Grace when we die we will ascend immediately to heaven. Are we then wilfully deceived?" he asked, raising a questioning eyebrow.

"You did indeed die in a state of Grace, my son and by right *are* destined to enter into heaven – *eventually*...but your..."

"What mean you by eventually?" demanded Richard, his voice taking on a belligerent note. The monk's bushy brows furrowed, he raised a commanding hand to stop any further interruption and continued, his voice taking on a steely tone. "Your soul is tarnished and stained, still bound by the desires and suffering derived from mortal and venial sin, and as nothing defiled can enter heaven, your soul must be cleansed and purified before it can be reunited with God."

Richard's mind swirled with the terrifying images of Purgatory that were to be found painted on the walls of every church in Christendom. "Purification by fire and torture," he grimaced. Watching Richard grapple with the horrific ideas about Purgatory that had been drummed into his head by the Church's teachings, Father Gilbert shook his head in firm denial. "Not always. Purification takes many forms – the holy fires being just one of them. Each soul undertakes its own unique journey through Purgatory in order to reach that paradise which mortals call Eden from which it will ascend into heaven." The monk waited, giving Richard time to grasp and come to terms with what he had just been told.

"So be it," the king murmured in a low voice. "But just tell me, monk, how long will this journey take? When will it end?"

Father Gilbert silently considered his answer. Richard had already borne much, but the truth could not be hidden from him. "However long it takes for all corruption to be expiated from your soul; how long that will be depends upon you – upon your deeds during your life on earth."

Richard's eyes widened, the muscles in his jaw tensed. Seeing uncertainty and apprehension in Richard's face, Father Gilbert knew that his charge imagined himself traversing alone through a vast and hostile landscape, undergoing numerous terrifying trials and tribulations. With a growing respect he watched Richard gather his courage. Resolutely the young king rose to his feet and with his mouth set in an uncompromising line, he turned to face the mysterious doors which he thought would be the starting point of his ordeal. "I am ready," he quietly confirmed.

The monk laid comforting hands on Richard's rigidly held shoulders. "You must not think of it as punishment, rather as a journey of enlightenment and growth," he said in gruff reassurance. "Now sit, take your ease. I must leave you for a short while."

Richard watched his mentor stride purposefully down the length of the enormous, dimly-lit chamber until he disappeared from sight. Taking an unsteady breath he slumped back down onto the stone ledge behind him and wearily dropped his head into his hands. For long moments he tried to marshal his thoughts but his mind refused to co-operate. Over and over the monk's ominous words repeated themselves in his brain... *'However long it takes for all corruption to be expiated... It depends upon your past life.'* Richard sighed deeply; his sins were great and many. His was a deeply tarnished and blemished soul. His journey of atonement through Purgatory would, without a doubt, be long and arduous. He did not fear the physical and mental trials he was certain he would undergo; it was the prospect of facing the unknown utterly alone that he dreaded.

Chapter 6

Purgatory

Richard's hand hovered over the bishop. "Should I move him?" he mused aloud. Seeing his friend's gaze swing towards his queen, the monk smirked inwardly, knowing exactly what he would do. Richard was quite unaware of his obsession with the queen. Whenever they played chess he would advance her and then manoeuvre her all around the chessboard, instead of utilizing his pawns, knights and rooks. He watched Richard slide her forward and with humorous exasperation reflected that, despite spending countless hours attempting to teach him the finer points of the game, Richard continued to be a truly terrible chess player. Instead of using that cool assessing brain to strategize, he allowed emotion to rule his moves. This approach was totally out of character for the man the monk had come to know so well – the scholarly thinker and leader of men, who had been England's last warrior king. Having been Richard's guide and counsellor whilst he worked through his penance to satisfy the justice of heaven for his transgressions, Father Gilbert felt he had come to understand him well, but there were facets of his character that still remained an enigma. Richard's journey to redemption had long been completed. Yet he was reluctant to take the final step into the next world. Something held him back. It was time to get to the bottom of his determination to stay here. The Guardians were becoming impatient.

"My friend, for my own selfish reasons I would delay your departure for as long as possible and will be deeply saddened when you leave but you must see that you cannot remain here indefinitely." Richard raised his head and looked inquiringly at the monk, a hint of amusement lurking behind his deep set blue eyes. "Why ever not? I am comfortable here...I lack nothing." He let his gaze range around the vast library that they were sitting in. "These shelves contain a copy of every book and manuscript ever written." I have been humbled and honoured to have been allowed to debate with and listen to the thoughts of some of humanity's greatest and most wise souls..." He couldn't suppress a chuckle. "And been amused by the cogitations of the most foolish....rest assured, monk, I am content," he murmured and, with a half-smile, slid his knight into Father Gilbert's trap.

The monk huffed in silent irritation but didn't immediately pounce. It would be more instructive if Richard had time to perceive his error before he made his move. He sometimes wondered whether his protégé deliberately played badly just to bait him. Nevertheless, Father Gilbert was determined that he should become at least competent at chess before their ways finally parted. "Be that as it may, but your period of atonement was completed countless decades of mortal time ago," he pointed out dryly. "No other soul has lingered so long here in heaven's ante-room..." And there it was, that flicker of resistance behind

Richard's eyes. The monk decided to confront head on his charge's disinclination to leave Purgatory. "You have been tested, undergone correction and cleansed your soul of every residue of sin. Why are you so reluctant to embrace your heavenly destiny?" he demanded.

Pushing up from the deep leather armchair in which he sat, Richard strolled down the length of the book-lined room towards the tall mullioned windows that dominated one end. His lean figure was delineated by bright spring sunlight as he stood motionless, gazing reflectively out over the lush fertile valley that spread out below him. A tiny movement in the muscles at the corner of his mouth was the only outward sign of the troubled thoughts that plagued him. Sighing, Richard turned towards his mentor with a quizzical look. "And what exactly *is* my heavenly destiny, Gilbert? What will I experience for all eternity when I leave Eden?"

The monk moved a pawn and looked up with a benign smile "Why, Richard...you already know what is waiting for you... absolute peace...perfect happiness."

Hearing the confidence in the monk's words Richard briefly closed his eyes *...peace...happiness ... for him...how could that be...?* He swung round and slowly retraced his steps down the length of the room. Lowering himself back into his chair, he studied the state of play on the chessboard; his knight was doomed and he suspected that his bishop would go next. With a mental shrug he accepted the loss of his knight and sent his queen to waylay the monk's bishop. Having made his move he sat deep in thought for long moments, then clearing his throat, he turned determinedly towards the man with whom he had developed a bond closer than friendship, closer than family. "You told me long ago, that once it had been made ready, each soul would know when the time was right for it to ascend into the Afterlife."

Alerted by the edgy tension in Richard's voice, Father Gilbert abandoned the game. Reclining against the worn leather back of his chair, he folded powerful arms across his deep chest. Stretching out his legs he crossed one ankle over the other and raised his sharp eyes to Richard's face. "Tell me what is troubling you, Dickon," he commanded. "What weighs so heavily on your soul that you will not allow yourself to find the heavenly repose you laboured so long and hard to achieve?"

Richard flinched at the monk's use of that almost forgotten diminutive of his name; he struggled to push away the vivid recollections of his past life that it conjured up in his mind. Resting his elbows on his knees, he bowed his head. His eyes absently traced the grain of the ancient wooden floor beneath his feet whilst he tried to marshal his thoughts and find the words to explain himself. Finally, drawing in a deep breath, he spoke in a bleak voice. "That's just the point, Gilbert...I do not feel ready to leave here...so much remains unresolved in my mind...I am not fit..." Richard's voice trailed off, he raised his eyes and the monk was taken aback by the depth of pain that he saw there.

His bushy silver brows drew together. "Sweet Jesu!" he swore silently in self-recrimination. *How had he missed this?* Feelings of compassion and guilt warred with each other inside the monk. Somehow he had let the young king down. Father Gilbert began to question himself... *Had he become complacent because Richard had undertaken every task and trial he was set with fortitude and courage? And yet...* having mentored and guided countless

41

transitory souls as they travelled along their personal road to redemption here in Purgatory, never once had one hesitated in this way, questioning the final judgement of heaven and resisting reunification with the Creator.

The monk pushed aside the low table on which the chess set lay and leant forward. "Explain this foolishness that has taken root in that agile brain of yours," he demanded gruffly.

Richard gave a hollow laugh, and with a grim twist to his mouth he began to speak. "My name is synonymous with evil. In the mortal world I am the hunchback killer king. The most heinous crimes have been laid at my door." In a flat voice he continued. "After Tewkesbury I murdered Henry VI and his son Edward of Lancaster. I executed my brother Clarence – drowning him in a butt of Malmsey. I usurped England's throne to which I had no right. I killed my nephews. I poisoned my wife in order to incestuously marry my niece. My place in history is amongst the most reviled and evil villains that ever existed. How can someone whose reputation is so mired in infamy find peace in heaven?" he questioned in a low, strained voice.

Sensing the deep anguish that lay behind them, the monk listened to Richard's words with growing concern. His state of mind was far worse than he had at first envisaged. A surge of anger flowed through him – why had Richard not come to him with his fears and doubts instead of tormenting himself for so long? The monk rose swiftly to his feet. Towering over Richard he began to speak but then his mouth snapped shut to hold back a threatening stream of reproachful words. Mutely shaking his head, not trusting himself to speak, he moved across the room to stand in front of the massive stone fireplace. For long silent moments he scowled down into the leaping flames then began to prowl back and forth, his rapid strides causing the skirt of his rough woollen robe to swing dangerously close to the burning logs. He stopped abruptly and in a voice made harsh with unease and worry for his friend, he snapped, "This…" He swallowed then began again. "This self-castigation must stop immediately!" From beneath brooding brows he scrutinized Richard's unhappy face. "Think carefully before you answer, Richard…which are you in danger of accepting – Heaven's affirmation of your soul's purity or the vile image of you created by Henry VII's propagandists and the Tudor chroniclers who curried favour with the paranoid, murderous dynasty he founded… Which should take precedence in your mind?" he demanded sternly.

Richard drew in a shaky breath, his mouth tightened a fraction at the censure and thread of anger he heard in his mentor's voice, but he raised his chin and looked the monk straight in the eye. "The truth of a man's reputation matters, Gilbert. In the eyes of all of humankind I am a soul beyond redemption."

The monk snorted impatiently. "It matters not how you are regarded in the mortal world if Heaven judges you fit to enjoy eternal life with God?"

Richard's shoulders slumped in resignation. "Cease lecturing me, Gilbert – I know you have the right of it…but it still torments me to know that throughout all eternity, I am fated to be the monster king."

Instinctively the monk reached a comforting hand towards him but then he hesitated and drew back as the realization dawned on him that throughout their long association, he and Richard had concentrated so hard on working to free his soul from all taint of sin, that in the process his emotional psyche had been neglected. In this unquiet state of mind he most certainly could not leave Eden; there would be no peace for him in heaven. The monk found himself in a situation that he had not foreseen, that he had no real experience of dealing with. He slowly paced the length of the room, vainly searching his mind for a way forward – a way to his ease his young friend's anguish.

A heavy, drawn-out silence descended upon the room, as each man wrestled with his unhappy thoughts. Richard shifted restlessly in his seat, his troubled gaze falling upon the abandoned chess game. He saw that he had exposed his queen, placed her in danger. Leaning forward, he picked up the tiny, intricately-carved chess piece and stroked it with a tender forefinger. She reminded him of his own delicate Anne...the dainty, playful sprite of his childhood... who was married against her will to that arrogant pup Edward of Lancaster, when her father, the Earl of Warwick, turned traitor. Whom he'd ransacked the stews of London for, after his brother Clarence had hidden her from him; putting her to work as a scullion maid in a cook shop, so that he could keep his greedy clutches on her inheritance...his precious love, whose frail, grief-stricken body had not the strength to fight, when sickness struck after the death of their beloved son.

Embers of the ferocious rage that had swept through him at the time, sparked back into life as he remembered Elizabeth Woodville's false display of grief during Anne's burial service. She had sidled up to him, shamelessly offering up his niece Elizabeth to take his dead love's place. Like the keeper of a brothel, she had touted her daughter's desirable assets – her fair, robust beauty and ripe youthfulness – *'Since the death of the Prince of Wales, you need sons now more than ever,'* she had pointed out with feigned sympathy. *'Elizabeth is young, fertile and docile, she will breed them for you.'* Her mouth had smirked lasciviously. *'The women in my family are renowned for their fertility, as I have already proven, having gifted your brother with ten children.'* She had been enraged by his curt dismissal of her distasteful offer and had turned traitor. Seduced by his offer to make Elizabeth his queen and the promise of her own return to a position of influence in his Court, she had sold her daughter to Henry Tudor. As Richard's lips curled in remembered disgust an insidious thought slid into his brain; he had been very naive in the game of power politics. He should have incarcerated Elizabeth Woodville in a nunnery as soon as she made her vile suggestion, for it was soon after she got together with Henry's mother, Lady Margaret Stanley, that the filthy rumours began to circulate – of his poisoning Anne because of an incestuous desire for his niece. Richard wondered what would have happened had he imprisoned Elizabeth Woodville and then smiled sardonically. It was rather ironic that after all her machinations her ultimate fate, in fact, turned out to be a lonely, impoverished incarceration in Bermondsey Abbey. She had not been able to resist plotting treason against Henry after the marriage had taken place and she found herself sidelined in a Court where his mother took precedence – even over the new queen. He sighed; one should not indulge in hindsight; it resulted in sadness and frustration.

A touch on his shoulder brought Richard back to the present. He looked up to find the monk gazing remorsefully down at him. "I have let you down, Dickon," he sighed heavily. "I should have recognised your feeling of unworthiness and not allowed it to fester and grow as it has done. I feel somewhat at a loss; not equipped to deal with the dilemma we now find ourselves in – you are questioning divine judgement and resisting the natural progress of your soul. I must seek advice from the Guardians – in the eons of their existence they must surely have come across a situation such as this before." He gave a rueful chuckle – "The mentor now himself needs mentoring." The monk's fingers briefly tightened in a gesture of comfort, and he turned and strode across the room. Struck by a sudden thought he paused in the doorway. Richard had received heaven's blessing and absolution but this rare and complex soul had yet to forgive himself! Resting his hand on the wide wooden frame he turned back to look at his friend. "To some degree we are all the masters of our own fate, Richard. Whilst I am gone perhaps you should re-examine the events that took place during the last years of your earthly life and ask yourself why you still consider yourself not fit for heaven. Why does the Tudors' invention of the demonic King Richard hold so much power over your mind?"

Hearing these softly spoken words, Richard's eyes widened. He searched the monk's face for a hidden meaning but could not penetrate its bland inscrutability. Could he bear to re-live that time in his life when his whole world had turned to ashes and crumbled away, when in the space of eighteen months he had lost everyone he most loved – his brother, his son and his wife? When, in the depths of his grief, he had underestimated, until it was too late, Margaret Stanley's dangerous obsession to place her son on the throne and his own vulnerability to the poisonous web of rumour, treachery and betrayal that she and her allies spun around him. With a sigh Richard rested his head against the high back of his chair. As uncomfortable as it was, Gilbert's advice was sound. The Guardians would not allow him to linger in this sanctuary forever. It was time to unlock the door to his painful memories. The soft thud of the library door as it closed behind the monk's retreating figure and the spit and crackle of apple logs burning in the hearth were the only sounds that broke the intense silence that descended upon the room.

Chapter 7

Middleham Castle – April 1483

The sound of laughter and high childish voices drifted through the open window. Richard frowned. The boisterous clamour was continually breaking his concentration but he was secretly grateful for an excuse to set aside another of the Abbot of Jervaulx's complaints about the villagers of Wensley. Dropping the long-winded missive onto the stack of documents that lay on the scarred oak table beside which he stood, he turned on his heel and strolled across the castle's document room to look down onto the tiltyard below. Training was obviously over for the day. In the watery sunshine of an early April afternoon, under the watchful eyes of his Master of Horse, the pages and squires of his household were enjoying themselves, racing to and fro trying to topple each other from their mounts with blunt wooden lances. He smiled with pride and fond amusement when he saw his young son in the thick of the action. Small of stature and fine boned like his sire, Edward was glowing with good health; full of energy and high spirits. Never for a single moment did he regret retiring from Court to live permanently here in Middleham

Castle. In the green hills and clean air of these northern moors and dales, away from the smoke and pestilence of the capital, his son thrived and the roses bloomed in Anne's pale cheeks. He was always uneasy in the sumptuous opulence of Edward's Court, packed with the Queen's Woodville relatives and their cronies, even more so since the death of his brother George. He now returned only when summoned by the king for meetings of the Royal Council and remained at Court for the shortest possible time.

Richard's jaws clenched. Charming, ambitious and incorrigible, George had been the instigator of his own downfall. Edward had made him Duke of Clarence, and Lord Lieutenant of Ireland but this did not satisfy his lust for power. All too frequently he had clashed with Edward over his policies and had continually dabbled in treason without any expectation of having to face the consequences of his actions. In defiance of the king he had married Warwick's elder daughter Isabel and then joined his father-in-law's rebellious attempt to restore Henry VI to the throne. After their reconciliation, and Warwick's defeat and death at Barnet, Edward had given George the earldoms of Warwick and Salisbury but his hunger for ever greater power led him to further treasonous acts. He blatantly usurped royal power by putting Isabel's lady in waiting on trial and executing her, having abducted her from her home and accused her of poisoning his wife and newborn son. Edward's forbearance with his unruly, unpredictable brother finally evaporated when George publicly proclaimed him illegitimate and accepted oaths of allegiance to himself and his heirs and then orchestrated a rebellion in Cambridgeshire. Convinced that George was plotting to take the throne, Edward arrested him and put him on trial. He led the prosecution himself, allowing George no opportunity to defend himself.

Even though his own relationship with George had soured, because of his attempt to stop Richard's marriage to Anne, upon receiving news of the Bill of Attainder and sentence of death he had rushed to Court to plead with Edward for his life. They were brothers – one blood. They had endured imprisonment and banishment together; the three of them had fought side by side for their family's right to the throne; and whenever it really counted, at Barnet and Tewkesbury, George had shown where his true allegiance lay. On this occasion, however, with the Queen constantly dripping poison into Edward's ear, emphasising George's treasonous volatility, it was a lost cause. In the dark of a murky February night in the dungeons deep beneath the Bowyer Tower, the private execution of his brother had taken place. Instead of having him beheaded, Edward had George drowned in a butt of his favourite sweet wine. He did not deserve to die in such a manner. The change that the Queen's malign influence had wrought on the King had shocked Richard. Gone was the astute, amenable and generous older brother whom he had idolised and honoured all his life, in his place he found an intransigent and suspicious stranger. Heart-sick he had returned home, the distance between them now so much more than just the physical miles between his brother's Court and Middleham Castle.

"A messenger has arrived from Westminster, Dickon." His wife's soft voice and the gentle pressure of her slim fingers on his forearm banished his dark thoughts. He looked down, letting his gaze caress her smiling face. They had been married for twelve years and still he never ceased to be astounded by her fair, ethereal beauty. Richard's heart lifted, every day he thanked his Creator for the gift of his precious Anne. With her mouth twitching in fond amusement at his abstraction and the look of entrancement she saw reflected in his eyes, she gave his arm a playful pinch, which turned into a slow sensuous stroking and gestured towards the doorway, where a royal courier stood ill at ease, clutching a leather satchel to his chest. "Cease wool gathering, my lord," she chided in a husky whisper, her voice trembling with suppressed laughter. "The poor wretch is most agitated. He will accept neither food nor drink, maintaining that 'tis a matter of the utmost urgency and insists that he immediately be brought into your presence."

Supressing a rising desire to whisk his wife away to their private chambers, Richard looked across the room and saw a palace courier whose anxiety was growing by the minute. Shifting from one foot to the other, the exhausted man spoke in a low, strained voice. "Your Grace, I come with a message from the Lord Chamberlain, which you must not delay in reading."

Richard raised a brow in surprise and beckoned the man towards him. *Messages about matters of State always came to him directly from the king. What business did their family's close friend William Hastings have with him that was so urgent?*

Moving stiffly, as if every bone in his body ached with fatigue, the courier came forward, dropped on one knee and held out the stout leather satchel bearing the arms of the Lord Chamberlain of England. Still wondering what Hastings could have to say to him that was of such importance, Richard pulled out the

51

letter it contained, broke open the great seal and began to read. *'The king is dead. In his Will you are named Lord Protector.'* His vision blurred, the letters danced in front of his eyes. He blinked fiercely and began to read again. His heart started to hammer heavily against his ribs, his head swam and a strange roaring filled his ears. *'By God's holy blood!'* he swore silently. *'Edward is dead! It cannot be so!'* He shook his head in disbelief. Grief tore into his heart. Richard drew a deep and painful breath into his lungs and read on. *'The Queen is enraged by the power the King has vested in you and plots your destruction. She, the Grey cockerel and the rest of the Woodvilles are crowing all over Westminster that they are powerful enough to rule without you and have informed the Royal Council that they will not wait for your arrival. They intend to crown the Prince of Wales in your absence. The Queen has already sent Earl Rivers and Sir Richard Grey to Ludlow to escort him to Court. The coronation is planned for the fourth day of May. Get you to London and secure the person of your nephew or your Protectorship will lapse.'*

Seeing Richard's sudden stillness and a strange blankness come over his features, Anne clutched at his forearm, giving it a little shake. "Dickon, what is it? What does Lord Hastings write?" she demanded, studying him with acute and loving anxiety. For a moment he stared uncomprehendingly at her and then his eyes filled with raw pain and despair. Needing to feel the living warmth of her slender body Richard pulled her close and pressed her hard against him, tucking her head into the hollow between his neck and shoulder. "Read for yourself, sweetling," he responded in a flat voice and put the parchment into her small hands. Anne's gasp of horror as she read of the

King's death and the danger they now faced, forced Richard's shocked and frozen brain back into action. He straightened, squared his shoulders and stepped away from her. Rubbing a hand vigorously across his chest to ease the heaviness of grief that lay there like a millstone, he turned to gaze out over the ramparts towards the vast open moors and the gentle wooded hills and valleys of Wensleydale. For many years as Lord of the North he had kept this part of England safe for his brother. They had been distant these recent years but he had never stopped loving and honouring his eldest brother and absolute loyalty to his king was the principle by which he had always lived. And at the very last, when he was dying, Edward had remembered this, placing his trust in Richard to protect his son and his kingdom. *'I will not fail you, Edward,'* he vowed silently. In a voice made steely with resolution he quietly declared his intentions. "I must ride south and intercept Rivers and Grey so that our mercenary Queen and the rapacious Woodvilles do not destroy us all and ruin the country."

A raspy cough from behind and a weary "If you please, my lord, there is yet more I must tell you," drew Richard's attention back to the messenger. Seeing the tired man still down on one knee he hastily motioned for him to rise and come closer. "The Lord Chamberlain has instructed me to inform you that he has sent urgent messages to your cousin, his Grace of Buckingham and to the Earl of Northumberland."

Richard nodded soberly in approval of the Lord Chamberlain's actions then gripped the messenger's shoulder in thanks. "You have done well. Go to the kitchens – they will feed you and find you a bed. Rest well, for you will be riding south again on the morrow."

"And will you also be riding south on the morrow, my lord?" Anne wrapped slender arms around his waist and rested her cheek against his strong back. "You must not delay, Dickon!" she urged. "Heaven help England if the Queen and her coterie succeed in their plans to rule the kingdom through young Edward! Honour, justice and fair play will depart this land forever and avarice, betrayal and false witness will rule instead. Nothing and no-one will be safe." Her voice sank to a harsh whisper and her slight frame shook in remembered disgust. "I was at Court when the Woodvilles had the Mayor of London arrested. Their henchmen dragged him out of his home and hauled him in front of the Magistrates on trumped-up charges. They seized most of his property and when the poor gentleman was eventually cleared and released they refused to return what they had stolen from him."

Richard turned, gathered her into the protective circle of his arms and kissed her gently on the forehead. "Hush, dereling. It will not come to that. God willing, and with Buckingham and Northumberland's aid, I will thwart the Queen's plans." Holding her face between strong hands, he gazed intently into her anxious grey eyes, his thumbs rubbing tenderly over her high cheekbones. "Do I not always protect and keep what is mine?" he murmured, with the ghost of a smile playing around his mouth. He watched a rosy blush spread over Anne's face as they shared the memory of him storming through the kitchen of the cook shop his brother had hidden her in; of him carrying her to his horse and riding with her to the sanctuary of St Martin le Grand, where he had kept her safe from Clarence and his mob until they were married. To make her his wife he had willingly renounced his claim to most of her vast inheritance and had surrendered the position of Great Chamberlain of England and he had never once regretted it – it was a small price to pay for the joy she had brought him.

He did not immediately ride south though. Before he did so he had to be quite certain that the Queen and the Woodvilles were in truth plotting to murder him and seize power. The very next day Lord Hastings' courier rode back to London with Richard's letter of condolence to the Queen, pledging loyalty to her son. He also carried with him letters to the Royal Council and Earl Rivers. Whilst Richard waited to hear from them, he strengthened England's northern borders by despatching veterans from the Scottish campaign to reinforce the northern Marches. James III's unruly Scottish nobles would most certainly step up their raids, once they learned of his brother's death and the accession of a boy king. When several days went by and silence was the only reply he received, Richard knew that he needed to act swiftly. It was then that the staging posts that he had established for his couriers, across the country to the north and south of Middleham, proved their worth. In a few short days Hastings knew when Richard would be heading south; a rendezvous with his cousin Buckingham had been arranged and the Earl of Northumberland had instructions to begin recruiting volunteers in readiness – should an army be needed.

Leaving behind his most trusted men to safeguard his wife and son, Richard rode out of Middleham Castle accompanied by only three hundred gentleman mourners. He would take no army into London to intimidate its citizens. Lord Hastings' man had recounted to him how, in a tense meeting between them, the Queen had insisted that her son be escorted to London by a large army and the Lord Chamberlain demanding to know *whether the army was intended against England or against the good Duke of Gloucester?* He had no intention of being seen as an aggressor in this crisis. However, his immediate destination was not London, he rode first to York. There he summoned all the northern nobles and gentry to the Minster to join him in swearing fealty to the new king and to celebrate a requiem mass for the departed soul of his father, Edward IV. As ever that loyal city did not fail him. When he appealed for volunteers to help save the King and the Protectorship, more than four hundred men mustered on the green in front of the Micklegate, pledging themselves ready and eager to do his bidding.

Finally, he was ready to ride south to meet Buckingham who was coming up from his Brecon estates in the West. They intercepted Earl Rivers and Sir Richard Grey at Northampton. There the true extent of the Queen and her followers' murderous intentions towards Richard were revealed by the discovery of the arsenal of weapons, armour and gunpowder that they were bringing with them into London. Once Rivers and Grey had been secured, he and Buckingham hurried to Stony Stratford where Richard took young Edward into his protection. They escorted him into London – the city was alive with alarms and rumours but the king's safe arrival in the company of his uncle, the Duke of Gloucester, and cousin, the Duke of Buckingham, surrounded by a group of courtiers in mourning for his dead father, swiftly allayed the citizens' unease.

Chapter 8

It was done. The Council and Parliament had confirmed him as Lord Protector. His nephew was installed in the Tower's royal apartments, preparing for his coronation, now only days away, and the first parliament of his reign had been summoned to meet immediately after the ceremonies had taken place. Richard's mouth lifted in an unconscious half-smile at the memory of the boy who had been isolated from his Plantagenet family by the Queen and whom he was at long last getting to know, solemnly pacing the long gallery that morning, trying to accustom himself to wearing the heavy coronation robes which had just been delivered. Richard let out a long exhalation of relief; the terms of his brother's Will had been carried through. He was bone weary yet his mind would not let him rest. He prowled restlessly back and forth along the battlements of the outer curtain wall. Behind him the rough stone of St Thomas's tower stretched high into the darkening sky; below the murky tidal waters of the Thames slapped rhythmically against the moss covered steps of the Watergate. For many the Tower was a threatening and fearsome place but for him it symbolised England's strength and stability. Since the accession of his twelve-year old nephew these had been put under threat by the Queen's determination to wage war for control of the boy. Richard leant over the ramparts and looked out over London's rooftops towards Westminster Abbey. On hearing of the failure of her bid for power, the cause of all the turmoil had fled into sanctuary there, taking with her as much of the royal treasure as she could lay her avaricious hands on. Dampness from the thin mist swirling over the river began to seep into his clothes. Shivering, he closed his eyes briefly and rolled his shoulders, his hand reaching up to rub the tense muscles at the back of his neck. Would that unscrupulous lady cease her scheming now that her brother, Earl Rivers, and his nephew, Richard Grey, had been taken north to Pontefract castle to await trial? Again and again his tired mind went back over the events of the past tumultuous weeks. His skin itched with the uneasy feeling that something was not quite right.

"Cousin!" Buckingham's raspy voice in his ear interrupted his pondering. He swung round to see Henry Stafford's set face and tight lips briefly illuminated by a slice of bright moonlight breaking through the shifting clouds. "There is mischief afoot. You must come at once to the gatehouse." Pushing himself away from the parapet, Richard muttered irritably beneath his breath, "By Christ's holy wounds when will I be allowed a little peace?" Then with dry humour he asked, "What is alarming you now, Henry? You are ever ill at ease and have spied enemies hiding around every corner since we arrived in London." A pained expression flitted across Buckingham's broad-carved features. "With just cause, Richard," he insisted stubbornly. "Follow me and judge for yourself whether I have the right of it." An edgy silence surrounded the two men as they strode along the walkway and descended the curved stone stairs leading to the squat gatehouse.

Through the barred window of a dimly-lit room Richard made out the figure of a woman flanked by two burly guards. Buckingham thrust back the studded door, which banged loudly against the stone wall making those inside start with surprise, and gestured Richard forward. Stepping through the low entry he was met with the smell of tallow candles, unwashed bodies and the sour scent of fear. Facing him in the smoky cell-like chamber was the tall, voluptuous figure of Jane Shore, his brother's one-time mistress, now the paramour of Lord Hastings. Richard paused. For the life of him he could not imagine why Buckingham had the Court strumpet under guard. A diverting thought made his mouth twist with sardonic amusement. The irony of the situation rather appealed to his sense of the ridiculous and he could not resist taunting his staid cousin a little. Giving a short dry chuckle, he turned towards his cousin. "Fornication is a crime in the eyes of Mother Church, Henry but not…" Unwilling to share in Richard's sense of the absurd, Buckingham cut in testily, "Listen to me, cousin…hear me out before you dismiss me." Henry's curt words hung in the air. Richard scrutinized his cousin's rigid features. Something was seriously disturbing him. After a moment he gave an imperceptible nod. Buckingham let out a long audible breath and began to explain the reason for his disquiet. "I have had little interest in Mistress Shore's comings and goings, since Lord Hastings took up residence here in readiness for the coronation." His eyes slid up and down her body contemptuously. "Except to laugh at the Watch's ribald jokes about his inability to go a night without swyving his Leman. However, some days ago, on passing through the long gallery in answer to a summons from the King, I happened upon the Archbishop of York and Lord Hastings in deep discussion in one of the alcoves. It was a tense conversation and they did not notice my presence until I was almost upon them. In that short moment I heard Mistress Shore's name mentioned in connection with some words that made me most uneasy. My disquiet increased when, upon noting my presence, the two men swiftly and loudly began to discuss the coronation ceremony. I gave no sign of having overheard them and joined in their prattling but that night I had one of my men follow her when she left Lord Hastings' rooms. I have had Mistress Shore closely watched ever since." Buckingham paused, his face hardened. A prickle of ice slithered down Richard's spine. He swallowed hard. "What were the words you heard?" he demanded in a thick voice. "And where does she go?" He wanted to shout at his cousin not to tell him, yet he had to know if what he was beginning to suspect was true. "Mistress Shore goes first to Hastings' rooms in the palace, then a short time later she slips out and goes to the Abbey sanctuary... and the words that I overheard were..." His cousin's brows drew together in concentration as he tried to remember the exact words. Then carefully Buckingham repeated back to Richard the words he had overheard. "*Mistress Shore will carry ...he succumbs... leave sanctuary...Regent'.*"

Richard stood very still; foreboding ate at his gut. Like an animal in danger his senses were suddenly sharpened and magnified. The gentle lapping of the river against the stone foundations of the tower became a pounding in his ears; the pungent stench of the human garbage that it carried out to sea assaulted his nostrils and made his stomach roil. In the lengthening silence Richard watched Mistress Shore surreptitiously wipe sweat dampened hands in the folds of her skirt as her frightened eyes darted around the room. Seeing herself surrounded by suspicious faces, she visibly fought back her apprehension and affected a demeanour of confused bewilderment. With innocent uncertainty she looked around the room. Dipping her head and curtseying deeply to him, she whispered in a low melodious voice, "Your Grace, I am at a loss to know why I am being held here."

Impassively Richard observed her growing discomfort; when beads of sweat began to dampen her forehead he allowed his expression to darken. Reaching out he caught her chin with hard fingers, forcing her to look directly into his face. "Your protector has no love for the Queen," Richard's voice dripped with sarcasm, "and you and the Queen have most certainly never been boon companions – your presence was tolerated at Court only because she wished to stay in the King's good graces." His voice softened with menace. "So tell me, Mistress Shore. Why are you suddenly so attentive, why do you visit her so frequently?"

He almost missed the shadow of guilty panic that crossed her face before she managed a look of pained surprise and respectful reproach. "Why, my lord, for no other reason but that the Queen is now a sad and lonely widow. We shared a love of the King and since his death she has been kind to me."

Richard gave a cold laugh. "Elizabeth Woodville is never kind to anyone without having an ulterior motive." He studied

Mistress Shore through narrowed eyes. The whore's fear was plain to see by the pulse beating erratically at the base of her throat. "What did she want from you I wonder?" he pondered in a soft sinister voice as he slowly circled her like a predator getting ready to pounce on its prey. Suddenly he snapped out an order, "I want her stripped and searched…every piece of clothing is to be examined."

The blood drained from Mistress Shore's face, she shrank back and gasped in horror. The sound of her distress halted him for a moment; she was an adulterous slut and deserved no such consideration, but he could not bring himself to expose the woman's nakedness to the lascivious eyes of the guards. "Take her into another room and find some women to do it," he instructed in a harsh voice.

The door of the cell in which Jane Shore was being searched opened. Richard checked his impatient striding and took a hurried step forward. "Well?" he snapped out.

The mistress in charge of the Tower's chamberwomen dipped a respectful curtsey and shook her head regretfully. "I am sorry, my lord. I oversaw the search of Mistress Shore's person myself and have carefully examined every stitch of clothing that my women removed. We can find nothing."

Buckingham straightened his stocky body away from the wall against which he leant, and crossing his arms over his chest he blew out a noisy, frustrated breath. "By Satan's forked tail I know not how, but that strumpet is concealing something," he exclaimed.

Glancing over Mistress Mortimer's shoulder, Richard caught Jane Shore's sly little smile of triumph before her face took on an expression of helpless, sorrowful endurance. Anger hardened his features. He would be damned if he allowed himself to be bested by this lewd, adulterous female. For certain she had been carrying something about her person and he intended to find it even if he had to tear every stitch of her clothing into shreds. He turned towards the barred window overlooking the river. His fingers drummed distractedly against the stone sill as he watched a Thames Waterman tie up his ferry and help his passengers onto the jetty below. "Bring all her clothes out here to me," he ordered grimly, "and then search every inch of her body once more."

Mistress Shore's clothes were in tatters by the time he and Buckingham had slit open every seam. Her face paled and her smirk disappeared rapidly when a length of withered root was found sewn into one of the long seams of her kirtle. "I know not what it is," Mistress Shore denied petulantly, shrugging her plump white shoulders when Richard confronted her with it. "Mayhap 'tis some dirt that got trapped there in the sewing of the garment," she suggested artlessly. Richard's apothecary identified it as Wolfsbane.

Richard rubbed his aching temples and gritted his teeth in frustration. Dawn was beginning to lighten the sky above the city and still Mistress Shore obstinately refused to speak. At the end of his patience, his cousin slammed a broad palm down upon the rough planks of the trestle table on which the remnants of Mistress Shore's clothes were heaped. "We have no other recourse but to use torture to make her talk," he snapped. The dungeon and torture were already on Richard's mind but not in the manner Buckingham envisaged. He had never yet used torture against a woman and he had no intention of doing so now – but only he knew this. He called the guard. "Bring Mistress Shore to me," he instructed. Clad in her chemise and wrapped in a rough blanket she stood stubbornly mute before him. He stepped menacingly close, and crowding her with his body he whispered coldly, "Tell me what you know, Mistress Shore." Wordlessly she lowered her gaze to the floor. He stepped away and shrugged his shoulders. "Then you leave me no other option." He turned towards the guards. "Bring her."

In the dungeon she remained intransigent when she was introduced to the master of torture. Her face took on a sickly grey pallor when he showed her the manacles, thumbscrews and the rack. Mistress Shore's defiance crumbled and her knees gave way when she saw the unholy glow of the fires and the caged rats. It was then that she decided that she was not ready to martyr herself for her lover. In a voice trembling with terror she confessed that for weeks she had been carrying messages between the Queen, Lord Hastings and his fellow conspirators – Doctor John Morton, the Bishop of Ely; Thomas Lord Stanley and Thomas Rotherham, the Archbishop of York. Mistress Shore went on to tell them that from tomorrow onwards, so that no-one would suspect poisoning, they intended to make Richard appear increasingly ill by putting small but ever greater amounts of Wolfsbane into his food. The Queen had demanded that Hastings do the poisoning as his closeness to Richard would allow him to easily slip the poison into his food and she also wanted him to prove his loyalty to her. On the day before the coronation Hastings was to give Richard a final massive dose that would kill him in minutes and in the ensuing crisis the queen would leave sanctuary and step in as Regent.

Richard choked down the bitter bile rising in his throat. Elizabeth Woodville's witchery had corrupted yet another man whom he had honoured and trusted. Hastings had been an unfailing supporter and close friend of his family. They had always been united in their love and loyalty to his brother and had worked tirelessly together these last fraught weeks to protect England and his dead brother's heir. Richard counted upon him as his closest ally. He expected murderous treachery from the Queen; the Bishop of Ely had always been a closet Lancastrian and Stanley was an infamous self-server; but the knowledge that his old friend was working with the Queen and the cohort of curs that yelped at her heels, and intended to murder him in this most vile manner, made his stomach heave. For long moments Richard was held immobile by the pain of his friend's betrayal. He struggled to breathe through a throat constricted by bitterness and grief but then raw fury roared into his mind. The desire for vengeance burned through his veins like molten iron.

Chapter 9

The muscles in his arms and shoulders screamed in agony and his body ran with sweat but Richard ignored the pain. Again and again he swung his heavy two-handed sword above his head to viciously thrust and slice into the Pell. Every morning since he had succumbed to a primitive urge for revenge and had William Hastings summarily executed on Tower Green, Richard had come to the training ground here in Baynard's Castle, his mother's London home, to try to exorcise his grief. In a few short days he had transformed the enormous tree trunk carved to resemble the figure of a man into a stunted, scarred piece of wood. The burden of what he had done lay heavily on his conscience. It had never been his way to act whilst rage ran hotly through his veins. As Richard leant over the hilt of his sword to let his burning lungs and pumping heart recover, his mother's pragmatic words echoed around his head. *'Cease this foolishness and stop punishing yourself, Dickon! Edward made you Lord Protector and High Constable of England. This empowered you to act as judge, jury and executioner should the monarch be threatened with treason. The proof was there that Lord Hastings and his conspirators contrived to destroy you. Parliament and the Aldermen of London are satisfied that you acted within the law. What is done cannot be undone. Make your confession and learn to live with your actions.'*

A gruff laugh behind him made him raise his head. "How many trees will have to be felled before you stop lambasting yourself, cousin?" Buckingham's voice hardened. "He had become her creature, her instrument of murder; of her intention that you should die in agony! He deserved his fate!"

Richard sighed and rolled his shoulders. Both his cousin and his mother had the right of it but he could not rid himself of the feeling that his act of retribution had been too hastily carried out. He should have put Hastings on trial before his peers and given him the opportunity of defence.

Buckingham clapped him on the shoulder. "I still think you showed too much leniency to the others. If I had my way they would all have lost their heads! But rest assured your orders have been carried out, I have Morton safely locked up in Brecon and Rotherham has been delivered into the custody of Sir James Tyrell in Suffolk." He suddenly sniffed and swiftly moved away from Richard. "Ugh! My friend, your odour is rather malodorous! You will need to bathe before presenting yourself to Duchess Cecily who wishes your attendance on her in the Solar."

Richard strode through the doorway of the cosy panelled chamber that was his mother's private retreat and breathed in the comforting spicy scent of gillyflowers that always perfumed any room she occupied. The morning sun streamed through the open windows, it shimmered across the beeswaxed floor and surrounded the waiting figure of Cecily, Duchess of York in a bright aureole of light. War and loss had removed the bloom from the Rose of Raby's legendary beauty. Having been robbed of a beloved husband and three of her sons, her lovely face bore the marks of pain and grief and yet an aura of warmth and vibrant energy emanated from her erect, slender frame giving the impression of a much younger woman. Beside her, somewhat diminished by her vital presence, stood the portly Bishop of Bath and Wells.

Richard swore beneath his breath, "God's nails! I have had a surfeit of bishops these last weeks!"

The Royal Council had gathered that morning in the Abbey for a rehearsal and final overview of the coronation preparations, simple, straightforward proceedings that did not warrant his presence. *'Everything was in place, nothing could possibly have gone amiss,'* Richard told himself but Robert Stillington looked decidedly ill at ease; sweat beaded his brow and he swallowed continually as if trying to ease a dry throat. The duchess's face lit up when she saw her only remaining son come into the room. Giving the bishop a nod of encouragement, his mother moved forward and extended a slender hand towards Richard, which he raised to his lips in tender affection.

"My lord bishop has an urgent desire to speak with you alone, your Grace," she announced with a disarming smile and then lowered her voice so that only he could hear. "He is sorely agitated, Dickon, he insists that what he has to tell you weighs so heavily on his conscience that it will not wait a moment longer." Cecily lightly squeezed her son's forearm then gracefully looping the heavily embroidered skirt of her gown over her arm, she swept out of the room. Richard smiled as the door closed quietly behind her. The Queen and her acolytes sneered at his lady mother's devotion to her dead husband and pride in her family, referring to her insultingly as 'Proud Cis,' but he doubted they could match her bravery and courage in adversity. Alone on the market cross in Ludlow, she had faced down a hostile army when his father was forced to flee following his defeat at Ludford Bridge. She had confronted king and parliament after their act of Attainder against the Nevilles left her destitute, shaming them into paying her a sum of money for the maintenance of herself and her sons. And when his father and brother Edmund were slain in battle at Wakefield, she sent him and George to safety in Burgundy and continued to work tirelessly against their enemies until they were routed at Towton and Edward became king. Ever mindful of her noble lineage, his mother was indeed proud and haughty when she deemed it fitting but Cecily Neville was also warm hearted, steadfast and loyal to those she cared for.

The sound of the bishop's rapid, anxious breathing drew Richard's attention back to the elderly cleric. He eyed him warily and waited for him to speak. Richard was somewhat surprised to see the prelate, who was ever conscious of the importance and dignity of his position, wearing the simple brown habit of a Franciscan friar. "Y...your g...grace ...the coronation... the boy is ... it must not..." The bishop stammered out a disjointed jumble of words that made no sense. His shaking voice lowered to a whisper then trailed away. Robert Stillington's shoulders slumped and he stared down at the floor. Perplexed, Richard watched the bishop's pudgy be-ringed hands pull and twist the folds of his robe in distress. *What in heaven's name had gone so wrong this morning that the old man went in terror of telling me?'*

he wondered. Then it struck him that since his brother's death, the bishop had in fact not attended any Royal Council meetings. *'Why then was he babbling about difficulties with the ceremony?'* At a complete loss and to give the distraught man time to compose himself, he walked across the room to the window. It was a busy day on the Thames. He loved watching the teeming river traffic. Heavily laden merchants' galleys ploughed their way sedately along, brightly painted private barges were rowed purposefully over the swiftly flowing waters and Wherrymen busily transported their passengers backwards and forwards from bank to bank – all intent on completing their business of the day. At length he turned back to the priest. "Come now, sir, if you have discovered some complication, there is yet time to resolve the problem." The silence lengthened. Finally he lost patience. "I'm listening, sir. Speak!" he ordered bluntly.

Robert Stillington gathered up his courage. Clearing his throat nervously, he took a deep, steadying breath and began again. "My Lord, the boy must not be crowned...the late king's marriage was not a true..."

Richard's bark of sardonic laughter cut him short. "Stop now! You surely do not mean to resurrect that worn out old objection!" he exclaimed scornfully, glowering balefully at the bishop. "It is common knowledge that my brother's marriage to Elizabeth Woodville was clandestine... that it took place in an unconsecrated church... without banns... without proper witnesses... and without the knowledge and consent of parliament and the peers of the realm." Richard paused and reined in his temper. "But you more than anyone must know that according to the laws of the Church if there is present consent between a man and a woman ... and Edward and Elizabeth had clearly consented to wed each other...then they are lawfully wed." He shook his head, totally mystified by the bishop's clumsy attempt to delay the coronation. Stalking towards the door he pulled it open impatiently and gestured for Stillington to leave. "Shocking and unwelcome as it was at the time and unpopular as the queen and her Woodville family still are, their marriage has been an accepted fact for nigh on twenty years. Do not raise my ire any further, sir, by continuing to seek for impediments to my nephew taking his rightful place on his father's throne, when there are none!" he warned in a hard voice.

Apprehension showed in every line of the priest's short stocky figure but he stubbornly stood his ground. "Please...your Grace...hear me! You are your brother's legitimate heir – not your nephew!" he exclaimed hoarsely."

In the frozen silence that followed this stark announcement, every tendon in Richard's wiry frame tautened in rejection and disgust. He swung round; with deadly intent, he advanced upon the bishop forcing him across the room until his back was pressed against the panelled wall. "You speak treason, old man!" he snarled, crowding him, the fury in his eyes battered at the terrified prelate. "I think age has addled your brain! As I have no desire to jeopardize my soul by harming a man of God I will ignore your ill-considered words, but if you do not remove yourself from my presence forthwith I will have you thrown into the Ludgate and there you will remain until you regain your right mind."

A shiver of dread chased down the bishop's spine but he was determined on being heard. In a voice cracking with trepidation, Stillington persisted, "Please heed me, sire!" He swallowed hard and continued. "Several years before he married the queen, I stood witness to a contract of marriage between your brother and Lady Eleanor Butler, daughter of the Earl of Shrewsbury. Lady Eleanor was a gentle lady of great rectitude and piety who refused to succumb to the king's attempts to bed her until he promised marriage. Although now dead, she was still living when the king married Elizabeth Woodville – therefore the marriage is unlawful and their children are bastards – a bastard cannot sit on England's throne!" The bishop's voice rose in extreme agitation.

As he listened to the man's shocking revelation the blood began to pound in Richard's temples. Grimly he scrutinized the elderly prelate's face, taking in the distress and fear he saw there. *Was he speaking the truth?* He felt a prickle of unease stir the small hairs at the back of his neck. "Why did you not come forward at the time of their marriage?" Richard demanded coldly. "And why did the lady herself not challenge Edward?" Expressions of guilt and shame chased each other across the ashen face of the Bishop of Bath and Wells as he stared silently back at him.

Long tense moments passed while he waited for the priest to explain himself but the bishop only mutely bowed his head... and then Richard remembered Robert Stillington's rapid rise to prominence at Court in the year of Edward's marriage to his sister-in-law. That year much to everyone's great surprise, his brother had elevated the unknown and unimportant Archdeacon of Taunton and Berkshire to be Bishop of Bath and Wells, then shortly afterwards promoted him to one of the most important positions in the Kingdom – that of Lord Chancellor of England. Richard's mouth twisted in contemptuous understanding. "Aaah...the rewards of silence...and what of the lady?" he questioned with icy disdain. He waited vainly for the bishop to answer him; when none was forthcoming he provided the answer for himself. "Of course... without your testimony, there was only her word against that of the king's." Richard's jaw tightened and he gave a scornful chuckle. "Edward was very good at extricating himself from unpleasant situations through threats and coercion. His carnal lust satisfied, she was of no further use to him. He would have left her in no doubt of the dire consequences that would overtake her and her family should she attempt to assert her claim." His mouth thinned with displeasure, and he gave the bishop a look of withering contempt. "That unhappy lady had no chance of receiving justice. She would not only have brought the king's extreme wrath down upon her head but her good name would have been forever tainted and any future marriage prospects damaged beyond repair."

In disgust Richard turned away from the wretched figure standing before him and paced up and down the room. "What became of her?" he demanded tersely.

Robert Stillington looked up, but refusing to meet his eyes he answered in a voice heavy with mortification, "Lady Eleanor retired to the convent of the White Carmelites in Norwich, your Grace." His breath hitched and he hesitated for a few seconds before continuing. "And died there four years after the king's marriage to Elizabeth Woodville."

Richard studied him with narrowed hostile eyes. "Why, after keeping silent all these years have you chosen to speak out now... what do you hope to gain from this astonishing confession?" he rapped out, giving voice to questions that were burning into his brain.

Under his implacable scrutiny Robert Stillington shifted uncomfortably. "I was already well past my prime when I stood witness to the king's marriage contract with Lady Eleanor," he explained in a low hesitant voice. "I never expected to outlive him and for this pre-contract and his unlawful marriage to become a problem for me to deal with." Drawing in a deep breath he straightened, squared his shoulders and unwaveringly met Richard's coldly assessing stare. "But now that I am faced with the prospect of his illegitimate son being crowned king, my conscience will not allow me any rest until I have righted a grave wrong and revealed the truth; neither do I wish to meet my Maker with such a sin staining my soul." There was a long heavy pause before the bishop continued, "Rewards and advancement were not the only reasons I remained silent, your Grace. Like Lady Eleanor's sisters, my family too was threatened." Slowly and painfully the old priest lowered himself to his knees. "I have come to throw myself on your mercy and to plea for your protection, sire. I am now the only remaining witness to your brother's pre-contract with Lady Eleanor and go in fear of my life. While the king was alive I lived safe under his protection, the queen did not dare to harm me, but since his death I have been in hiding, evading her henchmen with the aid of the friars."

Richard understood now the reason for the bishop's simple clerical habit – it was a disguise.

A mass of conflicting emotions raced through Richard as he wrestled with the enormous implications behind Robert Stillington's staggering confession. His first instinct was to order, on pain of death, the bishop's continued silence and to proceed with the boy's coronation. Stillington was, after all, an old man – he could not live for many more years. When he died the secret would descend into the grave with him and be buried forever. The temptation to pursue such an action was great but even whilst seriously considering it Richard knew it would be very wrong. "Get up!" he ordered, and catching Stillington's arm in a ruthless grip he pulled him to his feet. "Who else knew of this?" he growled.

The bishop looked with wary uncertainty into his darkly frowning face. "No one, my lord... only the queen...and then only latterly." He paused and thought for a moment then his face took on a bleak haunted look. "And your brother Clarence... we became close when I gave your desolated brother spiritual comfort after the death of his wife and newborn son. On one occasion I spoke without thought, and he gave me no peace until he had wrested the truth from me." The bishop sighed, his rheumy eyes became shadowed with sorrow and he spoke in a voice laden with remorse. "If truth be told, my lord, keeping the king's secret had become most burdensome, 'twas a relief to confide in his grace of Clarence but in doing so I fear I likely signed his death warrant, for as you know in his grief-stricken madness he rebelled and challenged the king's right to the throne. It was then that the king's pre-contract with Lady Eleanor became known to the queen. Her fury was terrible to behold. After his Grace of Clarence's execution she demanded another marriage ceremony but the king refused. He pointed out that their children would still be bastards and that it was better for the secret to be guarded by us three and for it to die with us."

Sadly Richard remembered how his own frantic pleas for the life of his brother had failed against the queen's malign whispers and demands for his death. The vague wording of the charge against George of *a conspiracy against the king, the queen and their son and heir...'* echoed through his brain taking on an entirely new and more sinister meaning. *'What have Edward's whoring ways unleashed upon our family now,'* Richard thought despairingly. *'We not only have a child heir but he is in all likelihood illegitimate.'* Revulsion surged through him. Elizabeth Woodville had persuaded Edward to commit fratricide in order to protect their sordid secret. After his death, knowing that fearing for his life, the bishop would seek Richard's protection, and facing exposure as his brother's paramour, she had tried to commit a double murder. She had sent men to hunt down the old prelate in order to silence him before he could reveal the truth and as a safety measure she had attempted to poison Richard himself. He knew that he had to act now. Richard's mouth set in an uncompromising line. "You are safe here, sir," he assured the anxious cleric curtly, "as long as you do not leave the castle." Once more he strode purposefully towards the door. "I am calling an immediate meeting of the Royal Council. You will repeat to them everything you have told me," he ordered over his shoulder and stepped through the doorway.

"Your grace! My lord! Please! Wait!" The urgency in the bishop's voice made Richard swing round. "With the aid of the good friars I was able to get safely into the Abbey for this morning's Council meeting...I have already confessed all to my fellow Council members." Then with the zeal of a reformed sinner shining in his eyes, Robert Stillington handed him their request to conduct an investigation and for the postponement of the coronation.

Chapter 10

D ay after miserable day rain fell steadily from the leaden clouds that blanketed the kingdom. It flattened the crops ripening in the fields and turned the streets of town and village into rivers of mud. Each morning with anxious and superstitious eyes the people from the highest lord to the lowliest peasant, vainly searched the sullen skies for a glimmer of blue. Saint Swithun's day was fast approaching; if this foul weather persisted there could well be forty more sodden days to come. The prospect of a failed harvest and a hungry winter began to loom large in their minds. With hushed voices and heavy hearts they whispered that the omens were not good for the new king's reign but then on his coronation day the country awoke to a hot July sun blazing down from cloudless azure skies. Jubilantly the citizens of London decorated their houses with bright banners and colourful tapestries. They thronged the streets and hung out of their windows to cheer excitedly and call God's blessings down upon the king as he rode from the Tower to his crowning in Westminster Abbey. The great church was crowded with an enormous assembly of England's nobles and gentry all enthusiastically determined to witness the coronation of the young king. It marked the end of long weeks fraught with alarms, uncertainty and the threat of war. When the Archbishop presented him to them and demanded to know if they wanted him as their Sovereign Lord, the thunderous roar of: 'yeah we wish and grant it!' that echoed around the abbey's ancient walls could be heard across the fields in the City itself.

Richard breathed a grateful sigh of relief as Francis Viscount Lovell lifted the crown from his aching head and Buckingham slid the heavy coronation robe from his shoulders. He watched his cousin reverently carry the purple ermine trimmed garment across the room and lay it carefully on the great carved bed that stood beneath the giant painting of his ancestor Edward the Confessor. His gaze travelled swiftly past the vividly dramatic battle scenes that decorated the thick stone walls of the sumptuous state bedchamber, to the far end of the long, narrow room where his mother and senior ladies of the Court were divesting Anne of her own coronation regalia. He scrutinized his wife's slight figure for signs of exhaustion or illness. She had been plagued by a persistent rasping cough since her arrival from Middleham and he had been afraid that her delicate constitution would not be able to withstand the rigours of the day. To his relief he could detect only signs of natural weariness; it had after all been a long, exhausting and emotional day for them both. A day full of pomp and ceremony, culminating in the magnificent coronation banquet from which, in the company of their long-standing friends and closest advisors, they had just retired. His heart swelled with intense pride as he thought of the way in which Anne had conducted herself this day, the delicate flush that tinted her alabaster cheeks being the only sign of nervousness. As his diminutive wife had slowly advanced down the length of the Abbey and knelt with dignity and humility before the Archbishop to be crowned, not one person there doubted that she was a truly fitting queen of England.

Richard crossed the room and stood in front of the wide, elegantly-arched windows that looked out over the meadows of Westminster. Daylight was waning rapidly; across the darkening sky, the setting sun was sending out brilliant streamers of saffron and vermillion. *'A red sky',* he thought and smiled slightly. *A sign that nature would be gifting them with another fine day on the morrow. Summer had thankfully returned to them after unending days of rain.* A flickering glow on the horizon above the city caught his attention. The people were lighting bonfires, not yet ready to stop celebrating the coronation of their new king. As he watched the deepening shadows of twilight steal stealthily over the fields a feeling of unreality crept over him. *'How came I to this?'* he asked himself. Never in his wildest imaginings had he envisaged himself as England's king. Unlike charming, ill-fated George, he had never envied his eldest brother nor coveted his throne. He had been content to rule Edward's blunt, plain-speaking northern subjects as Lord of the North. When the queen and her Woodville clan had unlawfully attempted to seize power after Edward's death, all he had sought to do was to protect his nephew but then Robert Stillington had revealed his brother's pre-contract with Eleanor Butler and events took on a momentum that spiralled beyond his control, leaving him with this unsettling sense of uneasiness.

Strong feminine fingers gripped his elbow, intruding into his disquieting reflections. "Tis a little late to still be asking yourself if you made the right decision, Dickon." The Duchess of York lifted one delicately arched brow and gave a wry laugh. "Besides there is no one to whom you can pass the crown on to. You are the only direct legitimate Plantagenet heir...George's Edward is disbarred by the act of Attainder; besides the poor child is a little slow... England would be saddled with another Henry VI if he was crowned. And the other two... are bastards," she sighed regretfully, "and Woodvilles to the bone, educated, schooled and trained by that accursed family."

Shaking off his unquiet imaginings, Richard turned to his mother, and the corners of his mouth twitched; she never failed to raise his spirits with her blunt logic and caustic tongue. He shook his head in mock chastisement. "Hush madam mother, subtlety and discretion must be your watchwords from this day," he told her solemnly with the ghost of a smile hovering around his mouth. "You are about to take your rightful place as the second lady in the kingdom – a status denied you for too long."

Tears gathered in the duchess's eyes at this long-delayed recognition; she blinked them rapidly away and studied the face of her youngest son who so closely resembled her dead husband. Cecily knew Richard still had grave doubts about what had transpired during these last three precarious months, so a little further reassurance would not come amiss. The duchess raised rueful eyes to her son's tired face. "I knew of Lady Eleanor, Richard. She was young, delicately beautiful and had been recently widowed when she came to Court all those years ago. She personally petitioned Edward for the return of her dower lands which the crown had seized because of some paltry fault in her deeds of ownership." She looked down and absently rubbed the silky petal of a white rose which was stitched into the ruby damask of her sleeve. "He was instantly enamoured of her. I warned him then that she, a gently reared noblewoman, could not be bedded and discarded like the light-skirts he favoured. Little did I guess that he was so possessed by his lustful desire for her that he would go so far as to promise her marriage." Cecily gave a derogatory chuckle. "It seems that Parliament in its investigations has now turned-up a further pre-contract...with an Elizabeth Lucy and another name, that of Elizabeth Wayte, is also being bandied about." She frowned deeply and shook her head in exasperation. "How many others are there? Who knows how long the line of Edward's pre-contracted wives will turn out to be?" She regarded him sombrely for a long moment. "Never doubt your right to the throne, Richard!" Cecily stated emphatically. "Do not forget, Dickon, that the Lords and Commoners' petition for you to take the throne was unanimous. There were no dissenters! Think of the thousands who came to see you crowned and to swear fealty to you in the Abbey today... of their great shouts of acclimation and homage." The duchess paused then and as if to emphasise her point further, she swept him a deep curtsey.

Richard gazed gravely down at his mother; slowly the shadows behind his eyes faded and the strain eased from his face. He reached forward and with quiet authority raised her. "Not so, lady mother...you above all do not bow to me!" he commanded roughly. Tucking his mother's hand into the crook of his arm he turned them both back towards the window. Drawing strength from her unstinting support, Richard gazed thoughtfully out

81

into the night, his eyes tracing the broad swathe of the Milky Way that wound its silvery path across the indigo sky. After a significant pause, in a low undertone he began to voice his misgivings.

"I do not doubt that by birth and right of succession I am England's king – Edward's rightful heir." His face turned grim. "But he has left a bitter legacy. My brother allowed himself to be ruled by his passion for women, the consequences of which are that his children are now declared bastards and for many weeks the spectre of war has hovered over the kingdom..." His voice dropped a fraction lower... "and has not yet entirely been banished. In heedlessly pursuing his carnal lusts Edward lost sight of his duty to England and the family, thereby destroying his own sons' chances of succeeding him and I now find myself in a role I never wished for, facing a destiny I never foresaw." Richard looked down at his mother with deeply troubled eyes that reflected his inner conflict. "And yet I cannot rid myself of the feeling that I have betrayed him," he added in an anguished whisper. He bowed his head momentarily and then straightened and squared his shoulders. An expression of implacable determination crossed his face. "I *will* rule justly, in the interests of *all* the people both noble and commoner alike." He paused and gave a humourless laugh. "I am, however, under no illusions. My hold on the throne is far from secure. For the present I am hailed as the saviour of the kingdom. The Woodvilles are so feared and hated throughout the land that the people are ready to accept any powerful ruler other than the boy whose family would ravage and plunder England for their own gain. But make no mistake, madam, it is as inevitable as night follows day that discontent with my rule will surface and Edward's children will surely become figureheads for dissent and rebellion."

"And how will I deal with these dangerous children?" Richard questioned softly, speaking almost to himself. Absentmindedly he massaged his temple, his brows drawing together in concentration. The duchess watched her son intently as he searched his mind for an answer to the thorny problem of her illegitimate, disinherited grandchildren, children who had been kept distant from their father's family, who were nearly strangers to her. "I can arrange respectable marriages for the girls and they will fade into domestic obscurity," he mused aloud. "And whilst they are still young, I can hide my nephews away in the North, in Middleham Castle or Sheriff Hutton. There my most trusted servants can keep a close watch over them." Richard shifted restlessly. "But the boys will grow into men... what future can they have... born and raised as royal princes – young Edward as a future king. They can be neither princes nor ordinary men. Will I ever be able to release them? Will they have to live out their lives as prisoners, surrounded by guards and high stone walls, never able to walk freely, to marry, to father children?" he reflected morosely. Richard's shoulders slumped as if weighed down by a heavy burden. Immersed in his melancholy thoughts he scowled sightlessly out into the darkness. Suddenly his hands balled into fists and his body tensed with frustrated anger. "By Christ's holy blood!" he swore viciously. "Would that Edward had controlled his lascivious lust for women or the Bishop of Bath and Wells's conscience had never pricked him to come forward!"

A shadow of alarm crossed his mother's face. Raising her hand she laid it on his cheek and turned his face towards her. "You will cease giving way to pointless doubts, Richard! Do not deny your royal birthright!" she commanded sharply, then her voice softened. "You cannot do otherwise than your duty, my son, you owe it to England and your family." Surveying him solemnly she called to his intense Plantagenet pride. "Would'st hand the crown to Lancaster? Margaret Beaufort's son stands ready and waiting across the Channel," she added slyly, anticipating his inevitable reaction to her provocative words. Richard stilled, his narrowed eyes travelled over her upturned face, then he gave a scornful snort. "His claim is flawed and weak. Cousin Buckingham has a greater claim to the throne than the upstart Earl of Richmond. His Beaufort line of descent from Edward III is through two sons – John of Gaunt and Thomas of Woodstock – and yet he has no royal aspirations." Shaking his head dismissively, Richard gave a cynical smile. "The much married Lady Stanley's royal ambitions for her son are foolish and unrealistic." Then all humour left him and his mouth set in an uncompromising line. "So be it," he murmured under his breath.

In that moment Cecily watched a transformation take place in her youngest son and she breathed a sigh of relief. His face took on an aloof austerity, his bearing an aura of power and strength. Signalling to his attendants that he was ready to retire, he led her away from the window. "Come, it has been a long and arduous day. It is time we found our rest. The queen and I depart for Windsor early on the morrow in preparation for our royal progress."

They made their way sedately down the length of the room, pausing every now and then to smile and acknowledge the bows and curtsies of their inner circle of loyal friends and supporters.

When they reached the smiling waiting queen, Richard bowed and raised his mother's hand to his lips. "I wish you a restful night, my lady mother." He lifted his face; fleetingly she saw the haunted shadows return to his eyes and for an instant his expression was unguarded. "Would that my brother's progeny were only daughters. If 'twere so, King Richard's reign would be untroubled by challenge and strife," he murmured to her softly. Cecily squeezed his fingers comfortingly and drew away. Catching Anne's small outstretched hand in his, Richard kissed her fingertips and led her from the room. No one took much notice of the silent courtier who listened intently, absorbing every quiet word of the low-toned conversation between the king and his mother; who watched them leave with a thoughtful look in his eyes.

Chapter 11

The noises of the great castle had ceased for the night except for the heavy, measured tread and low-toned conversations of the men at arms making their patrols. Wearily Anne climbed the shallow stone steps of the great curved staircase that led up to the solar. As she entered the bedchamber the dim light from the candle she held aloft flickered, briefly illuminating the shadowed corners of the room. The familiar comforting scents of beeswax, thyme and rose oil greeted her; she breathed them in deeply, allowing a sense of contentment to wash through her. It was so delightful to be home at last. A tender smile touched her mouth as she thought back to their arrival earlier in the day and their young son's shouts of joy and exuberant hugs. Their royal progress had begun immediately after their coronation, on a blazing July morning. Since then they had travelled the length and breadth of the country to show themselves to their subjects. Buckingham, as Great Chamberlain and Constable of England, had been left in charge of Richard's capital and their old friend Robert Brackenbury guarded his nephews in the Tower. Wherever they halted during those brilliant golden summer days, people had flocked to them, eager to greet and acclaim them as their king and queen. Every town and city in which they stayed feted them with lavish pageants and festivals, each determined to demonstrate their loyalty. As the weeks progressed and the hot summer had mellowed into the ripeness of early autumn, she saw Richard's uneasiness gradually disappear, giving way to a confident belief in his right to rule England.

He stood by the open window; the glow of a full harvest moon hanging low in the night sky outlined his strong, compact frame in silver. He did not turn and for a moment she thought he hadn't heard her enter. "Nothing has changed yet it feels as if we have been away for a lifetime." Anne paused, not sure how to explain what she meant, then she continued in a low voice. "It is we who have changed, Dickon – almost beyond recognition. We left Middleham so that you could protect your brother's heir and see him crowned and have returned as king and queen of England, yet everything here has remained exactly the same. It seems so strange, so unreal."

Richard turned; his dark eyes studied the slender figure standing in the doorway. She was so courageous...so fragile yet so strong ...had endured so much and was so very necessary to his well-being. Her quiet presence and unfailing support had saved his sanity during the turmoil and danger that was the aftermath of Edward's death. These last few arduous months since their coronation had been especially hard on her. Never once had she complained but he could see that the strain of constantly being on show, and of long hours spent in the saddle, had taken their toll. Her face was wan and drawn, the fine skin stretched tight over her high cheekbones. Richard walked across the room and gathered her to him, resting his cheek on her silky hair. "You are exhausted, sweetling, but we are home at last…here amongst our own people you can rest and simply be yourself…Lady Anne… not the Queen." He kissed her forehead. Here in Middleham, secure in their affectionate care, away from rigid royal protocol and the duties of state, she would swiftly regain her strength.

He began to lead her purposefully toward the vast, richly curtained bed that stood at the centre of the chamber but the tension in the arms that encircled her and an odd note of strain in his voice made her hesitate and lift her eyes to his face. Anne knew without a doubt that something was troubling him. Her small warm hand caressed his cheek. "No secrets, Richard…tell me." He sighed in frustration. He wanted her to rest but had never been able to hide anything from his too perceptive wife. The news from London would make all her anxieties resurface, but like the small, determined rough-haired terriers that hunted down the rats here in the castle, she would poke and prod until she found out what he was keeping from her. "There has been a fire at the Tower – yet another Woodville attack attempting to snatch back the boys."

He heard her inhale sharply. She was silent for a long time. "The Woodvilles will never cease trying to wrest them away from you, Dickon." Her voice trembled then firmed. "We shall have no peace until your nephews are placed well beyond the reach of their scheming mother and her supporters." Anne frowned as a further thought occurred to her. "And they need to be out of sight and out of the minds of the people – forgotten entirely."

Richard gazed down into his wife's earnest upturned face, his mouth curved with wry humour, and he gave a low laugh.

"Ever my astute Anne. I reached that same conclusion soon after we left Windsor on our great tour. With this in mind I have been in communication with my sister Margaret. I have arranged with her for my nephews to be sent to separate secret locations in the Low Countries. As dowager duchess of Burgundy and stepmother-in-law to Archduke Maximillian she has vast territories at her disposal where we can hide them away. In preparation for their removal, I had them moved deeper into the Tower – to the Garden Tower out of the public eye, where they could be more securely guarded." His mouth twisted. "It has proven to be a wise decision, made not a moment too soon... it was the inaccessibility of the boys that foiled this latest attack," he stated grimly. Richard's expression darkened with anger. "So many good men were slaughtered fending off those accursed attackers." A muscle clenched in his jaw. "I will take my revenge for this," he added in a deadly undertone.

The implacable intent in her husband's voice unnerved Anne. She shivered despite the warmth of the night. Trying to drive away the menacing stranger who had taken the place of her gentle husband, she buried her face in his throat and breathed a kiss there. "Dickon?" she whispered softly.

Richard started, his forbidding expression softened. Tightening his arms around her he finished explaining his plans to her. "All has been arranged in the utmost secrecy – only a very small circle of advisers – those whom I trust absolutely – are involved in these plans for my nephews and I would keep it this way... you will speak to no-one of what I am about to tell you!" he instructed emphatically. "When Sir James Tyrell takes up his appointment as Constable of Guisnes Castle, our fortress near Calais, the plan is to change the appearance of the boys and for them to depart with him as part of his household." He raised a hand and rubbed his temple abstractedly as he went over the arrangements once more in his mind. "Margaret's men will be waiting there ready to take them to her. Once in her secure guardianship, they will be given new identities and become pages in separate trusted households." Richard hesitated and stopped speaking as visions of the past crowded into his mind of that long-ago time when he and his brother Clarence were sent into Flanders by their mother to keep them safe from the vengeance of Margaret of Anjou and her Lancastrians. Now, because of their parents' ruthless attempt to place their illegitimate son on the throne, he had to banish these boys into what was in all probability permanent exile. He pushed away a threatening sense of guilt. "Perhaps, at some future time, when my reign is secure and the alarms and upheavals triggered by their father's death have passed into distant memory, I will be able to bring them home and recognise my brother's sons as royal kinsmen." Richard's eyes became bleak as he admitted to himself that this was a forlorn hope.

He scrubbed a hand tiredly over his face. "Come to bed," he ordered softly, "we are both weary to the bone and sore in need of sleep."

His wife's slight frame stubbornly refused to move; she stared gravely up at him. "There is yet more you have to tell me, is there not, Dickon?" she demanded, knowing full well that she would not like what he was about to tell her.

Richard sighed then his lips thinned in an uncompromising line. There was nothing he could do to soften his unwelcome words. Gently he stroked her cheek. Cupping her chin, he lowered his head and kissed her eyes, before his warm demanding lips moved over hers with exquisite tenderness. "This latest Woodville attack makes my nephews' removal from the Tower and into Margaret's care all the more urgent, dereling. The boys must be sent out of the country immediately. Sir James's departure will be brought forward. Margaret must know of the change of plan so that her men can be in place. I am leaving for London at sunrise." Anne's small stifled moan of distress stabbed into his heart. Seeing her eyes fill with tears, Richard wrapped his arms around her waist and held her tightly against him "Don't cry, my heart, I'll not be gone for long." He whispered the words into her hair.

She nodded despondently and sighed. "We have so little private time together, Dickon…and now that you are king… duty and responsibility will separate us even more…" Her voice trailed away. Wrapped in each other's arms they stood quietly together and gazed out over moonlit Wensleydale. In a sudden decisive move she turned in his arms, and raising herself onto her toes Anne put her lips against his ear. "Then we must make the best of the time we do have," she whispered huskily. Richard looked down to see naked longing in her delicate face; her smoky grey eyes held a sultry gleam and her rounded chin had a stubborn set to it. "This night I wish…" She paused; a rosy blush crept over her cheeks. "I had thought that we…it is time…" Her voice dropped away to a whisper. Modesty and extreme shyness made her hesitate and bite her lip. She had always followed his lead in their physical relationship. Determinedly she continued; speaking low and half-breathlessly Anne pleaded for that which

91

she had for so long desired. "Let me give you another child, Dickon."

Richard's blood chilled. Stepping back, he gently disentangled himself from her arms. He would give her anything but that. Giving birth to their son had nearly killed her. For years, to protect her from pregnancy as much as he could, he had been careful not to spill his seed inside her body. Their son Edward was healthy and robust. They were still relatively young; there was time yet to make more children. "Let Middleham work its magic and make you strong again, then I will think on it," he said placatingly.

"Then you do not want me, my lord?"

He heard the small throbbing catch of dismay in her voice and was undone. He loved her so and could not deny her... but he was determined, there would be no child from this night. He would rather have Anne alive than a dozen children. He ran the back of his knuckles down her delicately flushed cheek. "Would you like me to show you how much I want you?" he murmured, his voice little more than a husky whisper. She nodded slowly. His mouth swooped down to capture hers. Lifting his head, he smiled into her eyes and swept her up into his arms. Richard carried her across the room to the high bed and there he worshipped her with his body until the pale streaks of dawn began to lighten the night sky. Then he wrapped his exhausted and sated love in his arms and held her closely against him until she slept. Anne opened her eyes when the sun was high and found him gone.

Chapter 12

In frozen stillness, for long disbelieving moments Richard stared at the distraught man standing in front of him, flanked by his two captains of the guard. "Vanished... from their bedchamber?" He repeated Sir Robert's words in an ominously quiet voice. "Explain!" The word exploded through tightly compressed lips as he battled with the rage and frustration that surged through him. Taking in the rigid, forbidding features of his king, the Constable of the Tower swallowed hard, drew in a long shuddering breath and moved closer to the great carved throne on which Richard sat. Lines of agitation and anxiety seamed his homely face. "I know not how 'twas done, sire." His raspy voice shook slightly, the panic and confusion he'd felt on finding the two boys gone still evident in his speech. Even now he could not understand how his charges had been spirited away from under his nose. "I have the only set of keys that exists for the Garden Tower and they have never left my possession." His sense of having failed in his duty made the bluff northern knight garrulous. "The boys spent the afternoon playing in the garden... I'd had the master-at-arms set up targets and they enjoyed the sunshine, practising with their bows...young Edward seemed less melancholy than of late...the doctor's latest physic was at last easing the pain in his joints...the fresh air made them hungry... both ate heartily at supper time. I myself settled them down for the night and posted the guards." Realising that he was rambling, Sir Robert paused, and with the back of a trembling hand he wiped away the sheen of sweat that lay on his forehead.

In vain Richard fought to control his fury, his fists clenched and unclenched on the unyielding wood of the carved armrests. When it finally erupted his anger was a tangible living entity. It spewed out from him in violent waves and swirled around the panelled chamber to coil and snap around the nervous men facing him. Richard's icy penetrating stare impaled Sir Robert. "I put them in your care, trusting that you would guard them well," he growled. "Young boys cannot walk through stone walls and locked doors... someone took them!" The blood pounded in his brain; rising to his feet he began prowling rapidly back and forth. *'By Christ's holy wounds! Betrayed! A traitor...no...traitors! It would have taken more than one man to release the boys and get them away unseen... here amongst those I most trust.'* Abruptly he swung round. "And someone here is lying! There are traitors in our midst!" he snarled.

Sir Robert flinched but stood his ground. He lifted his square chin and looked steadily into his master's stony face. "It is not possible, my lord, the men are all loyal...have been in your service for many years...many are veterans of Tewkesbury and your Scottish campaign... I trust each one of them with my life... and yours, sire," he added softly. "Your nephews were never left unguarded. Yet when I went to wake them the room was empty."

Richard gave a sharp sardonic shout of laughter. "No traitors!" he spat out scathingly. "Then some magic power conjured them out of their locked and guarded bedchamber."

Sir Robert's ruddy complexion paled into a greyish pallor. His men shifted, eyeing each other uneasily as the rumours of witchcraft that for years had persistently swirled around Elizabeth Woodville and her mother Jacquetta of Luxembourg, sprang into their superstitious minds. Seeing fear and alarm growing in the faces of these battle-hardened men, Richard cursed himself for his carelessly spoken words. Breathing slowly and deeply he re-exerted his self-control and let go of the virulent emotion that was in danger of consuming him. Nothing would be gained by continuing to rail against what had happened. His nephews were gone, were now almost certainly back with their mother. Obsessed by her desire to rule England through her oldest son, she would now challenge him for the crown but he would deny the greedy scheming strumpet the opportunity to plunder his kingdom and tyrannize his people. He would defend his throne with the last drop of his blood! What he did not need now, when civil war once again threatened England, was for Elizabeth Woodville's supposed supernatural powers to be whispered about far and wide, striking fear into the hearts of his supporters. Grim-faced he swung round. "There *are* traitors amongst you!" he insisted with bitter certainty. "And they will be rooted out!" he added with sinister intent. "Meantime, you will ensure that none of the boys' guards speak of their disappearance. Your normal daily routine will be followed," he ordered. "If asked about my nephews, you will say they suffer from a slight fever which keeps them to their bedchamber."

Dismissing the two guard commanders with a curt nod, Richard's chilly regard returned to Sir Robert. "You are certain there is only one set of keys," he demanded, "and that you had them with you at all times?" The grizzled veteran knight squared his shoulders and drew himself up to his full height. "I never saw another set, your grace, and they never left my possession," he assured the king unhesitatingly.

Richard quirked a questioning brow. "Never...ever...?" He paused thoughtfully. "When you are in your private chambers... the keys are... where?" he asked softly and waited.

Certainty ebbed away from Sir Robert's craggy face. He recalled that whenever he retired for the night he invariably placed the keys on the large carved coffer that stood against the wall beside his bed. Swiftly he reassured himself, like most seasoned soldiers he was a light sleeper – he would have wakened if someone had tried to slip into the room, no matter how stealthily. Then further doubts crept into his mind...the nights had turned cooler of late, he'd drawn the thick curtains round the bed a number of times...and on more than one occasion he'd partaken of an extra cup of wine with his supper... He drew in a sharp breath, his honest nature had him admitting to himself that someone could perhaps have crept in, taken the keys and returned them without him knowing. Stricken with shame and remorse at having failed in his duty to his king, Sir Robert went down on one knee and dipped his head. "Sire..." he began to explain. Richard studied the unhappy man at his feet and sighed. Robert Brackenberry was a loyal and true friend. "Be not so hasty in blaming yourself, Sir Robert...there is yet no way of knowing how 'twas accomplished." His brows drew together in a deep frown. "What's done is done...we will know soon enough who stole the boys and how," he muttered darkly. Suddenly galvanised into action, Richard turned on his heel and strode rapidly down the length of the long room. "Get off your knees, sir," he called over his shoulder. "We must prepare for rebellion... The City needs to be secured and messengers sent to alert Northumberland and Norfolk that there is a threat to the kingdom so they can muster their troops." He stopped abruptly in the doorway. "And your most urgent task, Sir Robert, is to hunt down the traitors... question everyone...all must be able to give good account of their actions and movements in recent days...if they cannot... detain them...in the dungeons...an introduction to our instruments of persuasion will go a goodly way to loosen silent tongues." Richard's lips twisted in a humourless smile.

Francis Viscount Lovell rose abruptly to his feet, and with sudden violence he pushed back the chair on which he was sitting. "Christ's wounds!" he swore vehemently. "Nothing! We have been watching the Woodville witch for days...there's no sign of the boys...no unusual activity...nothing! Just as always she skulks in her gloomy sanctuary. 'Tis maddening, Sire! Why does she not act?" he demanded fiercely; the viscount's voice held the harsh edge of extreme frustration. Throwing up his hands in exasperation he stalked towards the window and glowered out over the smooth green lawns of the Constable's garden.

Briefly distracted by his friend's explosion of temper, Richard glanced up from reading Norfolk's report from the South and smiled grimly; patience had never been Francis' strong point. A moment later he dropped the despatch, letting it flutter down and lie amongst the maps and official missives that littered the surface of the massive trestle table around which he and his closest advisers were gathered. "Cease prowling around like a wolf being deprived of its prey, Francis," Richard commanded dryly. "Elizabeth Woodville is no fool. Her first thought, now that her sons are returned to her, will be to ensure that they never fall into my hands again. My nephews will be well hidden. She will not allow them anywhere near the Abbey." He rubbed his chin reflectively. "I would guess she will try to send them to the French Court... Louis is no friend of mine..." He looked up and saw agreement in the face of his Speaker of the Commons, Sir William Catesby. "We can do no more now but wait." Richard gave a cynical chuckle. "In her shoes I would not act until I had found a way to smuggle the boys to safety." He walked across the room and clapped the man who was closer to him than those of his own blood on the shoulder. "The Abbey is being watched night and day, everyone going in and out is stopped and searched... I will know if she or any of her supporters makes a move. Do not doubt it, Francis, we are as well prepared as we can be," Richard assured him with calm certainty.

"Aye, and we're watchin' the coast and all the main seaports," added Sir Richard Ratcliffe in his gruff Lakeland burr, coming up behind them. After a moment's hesitation he continued, "But if truth be told, Sire, with England's long coastline 'twill not be hard for her to find passage for your nephews on a ship sailing from some isolated fishing harbour. Duchess Cecily did just that when she kept you and your brother Clarence out of the clutches of the She-Wolf of France, after the execution of your father and brother Edmund."

Richard's teeth clenched at the sickening memory of their

heads, wearing paper crowns, impaled on spikes on the ramparts of York's city walls. *'History was in danger of repeating itself?"* he reflected with grim irony. *Except this time he was the pursuer not the pursued and unlike Margaret of Anjou he had no lust for such vicious savagery.* He felt no ill-will towards his nephews. They were the innocent victims of the chaos created by Edward and his paramour. "Enough!" Richard shook his head impatiently. "Elizabeth Woodville may well have regained control of the boys but it matters not...the Estates of the Realm – Lords, Clergy and Commoners – have declared them bastards. I, on the other hand, am anointed by God and crowned king by these same three Estates; if the Woodvilles move against me they are in rebellion against England's rightful king and will suffer the consequences. I have the throne and intend to keep it!" he stated with steely implacability.

Richard moved back to the table. Planting his palms firmly down on the polished elm, he leant forward to study an outspread map of London; an index finger traced along the routes into the city. "Guards must be stationed at all the main gates...even the postern gates must be manned." He looked up at his advisors as a sudden thought occurred to him. "Has there still been no word from my cousin Buckingham? It has been some weeks since he took his leave from me at Gloucester on a family matter, promising a swift return." An irritated frown creased his strongly marked brows. "'Tis more than time that he resumed his duties here... as High Constable and Great Chamberlain 'tis his task to undertake the prote..."

He was cut short by the raised, agitated voice of Sir Robert Brackenbury, followed by the forceful thrusting open of the

Council chamber's door. The Constable of the Tower came rushing through. "Sire, you must read this at once!" he insisted urgently, all propriety, such as bowing and waiting for permission to approach his sovereign, forgotten in his eagerness to place the folded piece of paper he held into the king's hands. With a quizzical smile Richard turned over the folded missive. Seeing Elizabeth Woodville's personal emblem imprinted in the broken wax seal, still surmounted by a royal crown, his mouth twisted; her arrogance was such that she paid no heed to the judgement of the Church and Parliament which had reduced her status from queen to Mistress Elizabeth Grey, widow of the country squire who had been her first husband. "And so the demands and accusations begin," he murmured beneath his breath, unfolding the letter.

Sir,

When your master tore away their royal status and made my sons his prisoners, he swore to protect them and to let me have daily reports on their health and well-being. For many long days, I have had no news of my sons. You as Constable of the Tower bear the responsibility for their welfare and safety. I beseech you to have a concern for a mother's loving heart, honour the promise made to me and let me have news of my children.

Elysabeth

Dowager queen of England and wife of the most glorious prince of blessed memory Edward the fourth.

Richard's eyes narrowed as he read the provocative language of her note. Incredulously he shook his head and read it again. "God's nails!" he swore furiously. She would have him believe that she was not behind the abduction of the boys and did not know they were missing? In truth, he should no longer be surprised by her cunning. He recalled the fate of the Earl of Desmond who, shortly after the revelation of his marriage to Elizabeth, had told his brother within her hearing that the marriage was unwise, *agreeable to your lusts yet not so much to the security of your realm and subjects*. Enraged, she had stolen Edward's privy seal and used it to sign the earl's death warrant. One corner of Richard's mouth pulled up in a grimace of disgust. He threw the letter down on to the table, his face darkening with an unreadable expression. "If in truth this is a genuine plea, then mayhap there is another, unknown player in this devilish game of 'cat and mouse...but I'll not believe it! There is not one honest bone in Elizabeth Woodville's body!" With a derisive bark of laughter, Richard turned on his heel and strode out of the Council chamber.

After long fruitless hours of searching Richard finally admitted defeat. There were no clues here in the heavily guarded Garden Tower to indicate who might have taken the boys but it could only have been his erstwhile sister-in-law's henchmen. Grimly he climbed the spiral stone stairs leading to the bedchamber his nephews had shared. Unlocking the solid wooden door Richard noted that there were no signs of it having been forced. He pushed it back on its immense iron hinges and paused for a moment, allowing his eyes to adjust to the dimness within. Walking to the window, he pulled open the shutters that kept out the afternoon sun; immediately brilliant shafts of light penetrated every corner of the room. The arched leaded panes were tightly shut and padlocked; it had not been used as an entry and escape route. It was clear that whoever took his nephews had been in possession of a key. Richard had no doubt in his mind now that they had received help from inside the Tower.

His eyes swept around the chamber. As he had directed nothing had been touched since the discovery of the boys' disappearance. The bedclothes were rumpled and thrown back. A crumpled linen bed-shirt lay on the ornate chest standing at the foot of the canopied bed, as if it had hurriedly been removed and tossed there by its owner. On the floor beside the bed a book of hours lay face down, the forced open pages creating a deep crease in its leather spine. *'Everything pointed to an abrupt and swift exit,'* thought Richard. Turning around he removed the padlocks and pushed open the windowpanes. The rich scents of early autumn, of damp earth mixed with late blooming roses and ripening apples, drifted into the room. On the trimmed and mown lawn archery targets stood guard over discarded longbows; quivers spilling their arrows lay beside them on the grass. His mind preoccupied with the contents of Elizabeth Woodville's note, he leant over the stone mullion and gazed out over the chimneys and spires of London. Below him, beyond the outer curtain walls, the scramble and scurry of city life continued on its relentless path. Richard's brow furrowed. *Was he perhaps being too hasty in dismissing it as one of her conniving tricks? Could it after all be a true entreaty for news of her sons?* For all her avarice and self-serving, there was no denying that Elizabeth Woodville was a loving, caring mother to all her children, doting especially on her sons.

The tall, powerful frame of Francis Viscount Lovell silently settled itself next to Richard. Deep in brooding reflection, the king continued to stare unseeingly into the distance. Francis' shrewd eyes scrutinized his face. He was relieved to see that the rage, which intermittently threatened to engulf Richard during these crisis-ridden hours, had at last burnt itself out. His friend's logical soldier's brain was once more in control. The viscount leant back against the rough stone wall behind him and decided to keep his counsel for the moment. The jangling cacophony of church bells tolling the canonical hour of Nones all over the city finally broke through Richard's reverie. Recognising that it was exactly what he had been guilty of, Richard muttered in a voice full of self-derision, "'Tis a great temptation to dismiss her note as a trick." Then with further self-mockery he added, "But methinks 'twould indeed be an entirely foolish action." Turning away from the window he regarded his friend with sombre eyes. "Tell me Francis, who, apart from the Woodvilles, profits from the abduction of my nephews?"

After a moment's reflection the viscount pushed himself away from the wall. Here was the opportunity that he had been waiting for. It was time to make Richard aware of the suspicions he had been harbouring for some little while. What he was about to say would in all likelihood not sit well with him. It would add to the anger and sense of betrayal from which he was already suffering. Francis knew the king would have difficulty in believing him but was determined that Richard would hear him out. His long legs began to pace steadily up and down the room. "My Lord..."

"Cease 'my lording' me! We are alone!" Richard ordered irritably.

A rueful smile pulled at the corners of the viscount's generous mouth. "Alas, I keep forgetting that my boyhood mentor is now two men...my friend Dickon when we are private and my lord the king in company." He gave a soft chuckle then paused. Distractedly, he combed back the unruly chestnut curls that clustered over his broad brow and became silent and motionless; totally immersed in his own thoughts. At last in a voice from which all humour had vanished, he gave Richard his answer. "There are of course those of your brother's disaffected courtiers who oppose you but also loathe the Woodvilles. Possession of your nephews gives them a focus for any rebellion they have planned."

His jaw tightening momentarily, Richard nodded his agreement.

Francis bent down and picked up the discarded book of hours that lay at his feet. Leafing through it pensively he continued, "And then there is our old friend the Bishop of Ely..." A note of distaste entered his voice... "who changes his allegiance as often as he changes his gorgeous vestments but there is no doubt that deep in his devious soul, John Morton is a rabid Lancastrian who harbours an intense and abiding hatred of the house of Plantagenet." Francis lapsed into silence, then began to speak again. "'Tis my belief that the slippery prelate would make a pact with the devil, if it would bring about the destruction of your family." Throwing the book down onto the bed he once more resumed his pacing. "Ely's record of loyalty speaks for itself," he added with heavy irony, his mouth twisting with contempt. "He sided with Lancaster until Towton. On being declared a traitor his glib tongue seduced a pardon out of your brother." For a split second a look of amusement crossed the viscount's face. He swung around. "Mayhap you recall your own witty observations about Morton's 'eloquence of speech' at the time, Dickon? They gave rise to much merriment at Court at his expense, which did not sit well with him for the bishop is a man who likes to be taken very seriously." Satisfied by the flash of reciprocated humour that he saw in Richard's features, he returned to his summing up of the bishop's treasonous career. "Having inveigled himself into Edward's good graces with his grave and honest countenance," Francis continued, unable to contain his sarcasm, "Morton then betrayed Edward by throwing in his lot with Warwick and Clarence's rebellion. He worked tirelessly to bring about an alliance between them, the Lancastrians and Louis XI to restore Henry VI. He was successful, as you well know, and your brother was driven from the throne... but, God be thanked, not for long," the viscount concluded, a note of satisfaction briefly softening his grim voice before it hardened again. "On finding himself once more on the losing side after Tewkesbury, our calculating friend persuaded Archbishop Bourchier to mediate for him and was pardoned again." The viscount's thick straight brows drew together and he grimaced. "From then onwards, Ely was very astute and extremely careful in the way he conducted himself, managing to convince your brother to trust him again – so far as to elevate him to the royal Council and make him one of the executors of his Will. After Edward's death he immediately supported the Woodvilles against you in their attempt to grab power for themselves – think on't, Dickon, until

Elizabeth married your brother, the family had been staunchly Lancastrian for generations!" Francis' voice trailed away as if rendered speechless by the bishop's record of perfidious plotting but then continued on a harsh angry note. "And when they were foiled he collaborated with Elizabeth Woodville in her plot to poison you... this duplicitous priest's smooth, viperous tongue persuaded Hastings, that most loyal friend and servant to you and your family, to turn traitor!" he exclaimed disgustedly. Francis' tall frame shuddered with the recollection of how close the plotters had come to killing his king and friend. Stopping abruptly in mid-stride, he took an urgent step towards Richard. "Heed my words, Dickon; you underestimate the bishop at your peril! Morton will do his utmost to turn your friends into your enemies whenever and wherever he sees an opportunity to..."

"I hear you, Francis!" Richard's sharp interjection broke into the viscount's rapid flow of words. "I am not unaware of Ely's predilection for betrayal but he is no longer in a position to do me harm," he added in a softer voice. "I have rendered him powerless. Buckingham has him imprisoned in Brecknock Castle."

At these words the frown between the viscount's eyes deepened, and his demeanour took on a grimness that Richard was unaccustomed to seeing in him. With a distinct hardening of his features he challenged the king. "That is not entirely true, Sire," he said, his manner suddenly formal, his lips set in an uncompromising line. "It is the opinion of the majority of your Council, my lord, that you imposed far too lenient a sentence upon the treacherous Bishop of Ely." He sighed, the sombre lines of his face sharpening with concern. "You, like your brother before you, have ever been squeamish about punishing men of the church appropriately – in accordance with the seriousness of their crimes. Morton knows this and feels himself unthreatened by any serious retribution; he will never cease to plot against you."

"How so? He is under lock and key!" Richard flashed back at him, his narrowed eyes probing Francis with a penetrating stare. The viscount gave the king a humourless smile. Moving to the end of the bed he sank down on the oak chest standing at its foot and dropped his forehead into his hands. "By the Rood, Dickon!" he cursed with quiet exasperation. "You are far too trusting. Have you not kept yourself informed about what goes on at Brecknock? Know you not that all the world is able to visit the bishop of Ely there? His sentence of imprisonment is a mockery. Morton is treated like a guest not a prisoner, he has the run of the castle. There are no restrictions on who is allowed to visit him."

"Seemingly Cousin Buckingham suffers from the same malady as I in not wishing to discomfort the cleric too much."

Hearing the king's derisory murmur the viscount raised his head abruptly and looked up at Richard, his eyes blazing with sudden anger. "The earl of Richmond's ambitious mother, Lady Stanley, and her self-serving husband, both still under suspicion for their connection to the Woodville witch's plot to poison you, visit him regularly! Furthermore there are no attempts to censor the bishop's correspondence."

Francis watched Richard absorb what he had just revealed. Richard's head snapped up and he stalked towards him. "And you know all this how?" he demanded bluntly.

"When you placed the bishop in your cousin's custody I planted some of my men amongst the guards at Brecknock castle; I am kept informed of what happens there by regular courier," the viscount replied.

"And you did this without my knowledge," admonished Richard. "Why?"

Francis stood up and rolled his shoulders, trying to ease some of the tension in his neck. "To protect you, Dickon... I feared your sense of loyalty towards Buckingham would get in the way of allowing me to place my spies in his household. Morton is clever and dangerous, he needs to be watched closely at all times. His so-called imprisonment will not have deterred him from working to achieve his ambition for a Lancastrian king to occupy England's throne once more." His eyes searched Richard's face trying to gauge his reaction but the king's closed expression gave nothing away.

Behind its impassive mask, Richard's brain seethed with Francis' revelations. His fingers abruptly stopped playing with the heavy gold collar of York roses that lay across his chest, as an understanding of what his friend was leading up to, filtered into his mind. His eyes locked with the viscount's. "Are you telling me that you think the bishop is behind the abduction of my nephews?" Richard scrutinized his friend's face trying to read his thoughts. "What possible use would the bishop have for two bastard Plantagenet boys?"

Francis gazed solemnly back at him, waiting until he found the answer for himself. The king scowled, massaging the back of his neck in concentration. "By God's holy son!" he whispered suddenly under his breath as the realization dawned on him that Morton had more than one motive for abducting his nephews. *Ely could use them to control Elizabeth Woodville and her supporters. Once it was seen that power had shifted away from them, alliances could be forged with other dissenters to create a cohesive rebel opposition to wage war against me.'* Richard gave a low scornful growl. *'Even if the bishop successfully cobbled together an alliance to oppose me and it succeeded in defeating me, it would not achieve his ultimate ambition of a Lancastrian England. The boys are Plantagenets.'*

"Have you worked out the answers yet?" Francis' voice broke into his swirling thoughts. For several minutes the king gazed silently at his friend, then a strange little smile hovered around his mouth. "Having defeated me he could of course follow my example...keep them shut up in the Tower... but whereas I will eventually release them and recognise them as kin, Morton will keep them imprisoned for the rest of their lives after he has manoeuvred that self-styled Lancastrian heir, the earl of Richmond, onto the throne." He stopped speaking abruptly, his body tensed and his hands clenched into fists as the ghastly realization filtered into his mind that as well as being tools to achieve Ely's ambitions the boys also stood in the way of them. Once they were of no further use to him, the bishop would have to dispose of them as they would be a constant Plantagenet threat. "Holy Mary Francis! If the boys have been abducted by Morton's henchmen we must find them and get them back at all costs!"

"You nearly have the right of it," the viscount confirmed softly, "but despite Henry Tudor and his mother proclaiming his Lancastrian pedigree long and loud he is not the sole Lancastrian heir. There is another who has a stronger, more legitimate claim… look a little closer to home, Dickon."

Totally perplexed, Richard gazed uncomprehendingly at Francis. Then slowly his expression turned into one of astonished incredulity. Finally, throwing back his head he roared with laughter. "By the virgin!" he swore, shaking his head. "Are you telling me that you seriously think Cousin Buckingham could also be involved in the abduction of my nephews!" Richard couldn't contain his mirth. "You are surely jesting, Francis!" He quickly suppressed his disbelieving laughter when he looked into the sombre, unsmiling face of his friend. "You would truly have me believe that Henry is in league with the bishop and intends to make a bid for my throne?" he demanded.

Richard's instinct was to instantly deny any such possibility. "What is making you so suspicious of him? From the outset Henry has been my most stalwart supporter. He discovered and alerted me to the poison plot and calmed the City's panic after the execution of Hastings." Richard paused, his nostrils flared on a sharp inhalation of breath as the name conjured up the bitter memory of the way in which the man whom he had trusted above all others had turned traitor.

"Are you entirely certain of his loyalty, Dickon?" demanded Francis. The king stared into the viscount's grim face and knew he would be unwise to ignore his friend's doubts. Suddenly resolute, Richard strode towards the door. "Come, Francis. The Constable keeps a goodly stock of spiced Spanish Granarde in his apartments. We will be comfortable and you will explain to me your distrust of my cousin."

The viscount stretched out his long legs and leant his head

against the high carved back of his chair. Taking a deep swallow of wine he ran a thoughtful finger around the rim of the silver goblet he held balanced on his chest. "Buckingham has every reason to hate both the Plantagenets and the Woodvilles." His eyes met Richard's across the empty hearth of the great fireplace that dominated the small panelled chamber in which they sat. The king shifted forward in his chair and surveyed him intently. "And how come you to this conclusion?" he demanded in a low tone.

Francis hesitated for a moment then drained the cup. "Think on't for a moment, Dickon...he is of royal descent. His ancestry like yours goes back to Edward III and he has Lancastrian as well as Plantagenet bloodlines..."

"Not a sufficient reason to doubt his loyalty," Richard broke in.

"Aye but the family has been loyal to Lancaster for generations," the viscount reminded him.

He stiffened as a flicker of surprise ran through him. "I had forgotten that," he muttered half to himself. Mulling over Francis's words Richard idly contemplated the frenetic dance of dust motes caught by the rays of the afternoon sun shining through the window and recalled that both Cousin Henry's father and grandfather had fought for Lancaster.

Seeing his friend's brows pull together in a fleeting frown and his expression become sombre, Francis persevered. "Your brother Edward disliked and distrusted him. He recognised the potential danger that your cousin represented to his crown, especially after Buckingham adopted the arms of his great grandsire Thomas of Woodstock. He kept him at Court, powerless and without influence, where he could be watched... Edward withheld the de Bohun legacy from him for good reason... because it would recognize and legitimise Buckingham's rights to the throne." The viscount hesitated, carefully considering his next words. "I know Buckingham is pressing you hard to hand it over to him and you are inclined to do so as a reward for his support but it would be a grave mistake, Richard."

The words hung in the air between them. Francis waited and wondered whether he had overstepped the boundary, between a king and his subject, something that had not existed between them before. When Richard raised his chin in a silent gesture that he should continue, he cleared his throat and carried on. "Now think yourself in his place, Dickon...imagine the frustration and humiliation Buckingham must have felt, seeing men of far lesser rank being trusted and appointed to high office...and then there is the humiliation of Buckingham's forced marriage to a woman far inferior to him in status. Think you that Buckingham is grateful to Elizabeth Woodville for foisting her low-born sister Katherine upon him when he was a minor in her guardianship?" Francis asked with mild sarcasm.

Richard rose from his chair and crossed the room. He refilled his goblet from a flagon that stood on a small oak table beneath the window and pensively swirled the rich ruby liquid around the silver cup. Lifting it to his lips he downed the contents and turned to face the viscount. "Before Edward's death I took little note of Cousin Henry," he mused. "At Court he was always there in the background...in my presence he was ever the urbane, affable courtier." Richard's mouth curved into a sardonic smile. "I do remember though that he did not give a good account of himself during Edward's French campaign. He proved to be useless as a military commander – we sent him home. I assumed he held no high office because he had no inclination to do so..."

The viscount gave a short bark of laughter. "Edward would not allow it!" he interjected forcefully. "He was always suspicious of Buckingham, whom he regarded as standing too close to the throne for comfort!" The implication behind his words was not lost on Richard. "You were taken up with your duties as Lord of the North and spent little time at Court... truth be told you do not really know Buckingham well at all, Dickon... in reality you have only ever had passing acquaintance with him... I as Edward's ward, on the other hand, have had greater opportunities to watch him closely over the years...your cousin is ambitious, he craves power and resents having been sidelined for so long. He is also very adept at hiding his true feelings...he allows people to see only what he wishes them to see."

Richard thought for a moment. "There was one instance when he was in a position of importance... Edward appointed him High Steward of England during our brother Clarence's trial...Henry pronounced the sentence of death. Now that I think on't Edward rescinded that appointment immediately after the trial."

Francis nodded. "Another log to fuel the fire of your cousin's resentment ...Edward's death was his perfect opportunity to curry your favour and grasp power – perhaps reach for the throne itself."

Richard walked slowly back to the fireplace. Leaning forward he gripped the mantle and gazed down into the empty hearth. His mind spun with the doubts and suspicions Francis had voiced. *Was his trust misplaced in Henry? Was he, as Francis insisted, a devious self-server set to betray him?* He reflected on what he knew about his cousin. Henry was indolent...did not like to exert himself... preferred life at Court rather than personally overseeing his vast holdings. He allowed subordinates to carry out his responsibilities. Richard thought about Buckingham's actions over the past months; rarely did he act on his own initiative, preferring rather to wait for instructions. His cousin was a follower not a leader. "No!" He gave a derisive snort. "He has neither the wit nor the energy to plot and plan rebellion!" Richard flung the words adamantly over his shoulder.

Francis rose from his chair and stood beside the king. "You are right, Dickon," he agreed softly, "but John Morton makes up for what is lacking in Buckingham... he has been in your cousin's custody at Brecknock Castle for months and in this instance Buckingham has taken his responsibility most seriously; he has been a most diligent custodian, visiting Brecknock frequently. Think you that Ely has not been whispering in your cousin's ear?" The viscount waited for his words to sink in, then continued. "Think, Richard! Direct and legitimate Plantagenet heirs to the throne are now almost as depleted as the Lancastrian claimants...Edward's children are bastards; Clarence's children are under Attainder. Who is left..? You and your son... If you are eliminated, Buckingham's way is clear...only Richmond and his weak and flawed claim stands in his path. Morton will almost certainly have pointed this out to Buckingham."

In the ensuing silence Francis exhaled slowly, and thought back to Buckingham's latest gloating boast about the extent and reach of his power – *that there were now more 'Stafford Knots' at*

Court than Warwick at the height of his power ever had 'Ragged Staffs'. He had had his say; it was now up to Richard.

The king turned towards him. "There is but one way to resolve this," he said sombrely. "I need to confront my cousin face to face with these suspicions..." A frown appeared between Richard's eyes. "Although of late catching up with Henry is proving to be a somewhat onerous undertaking ...my couriers seem always to be just one step behind him." The viscount slanted a quick look at him. "Not so this time, Dickon... Buckingham was here in London only days before your own arrival...when he left I had him followed...he is presently in Kent, at Penshurst Place... only a few hours ride from here... should he leave my men will follow him. Give the order and he can be brought here by daybreak."

Richard sighed. He had no choice, he had to know the truth. The prospect of another betrayal made the bile rise in his throat. "Do it!" he ordered wearily. Briefly bowing his head in acknowledgement, Francis strode to the door. As he stepped through pulling it closed behind him Richard called him back. "No! Wait!" he ordered urgently. "I want honest answers from Buckingham. If, as you say he is a practised dissembler, I would read his face when he is unaware, before he can conceal his true self. Sending men to escort him here will forewarn him... We will pay my cousin an unannounced visit but first I will pay a visit to the abbey sanctuary and speak with Elizabeth Woodville."

Chapter 13

A mile from the house they dismounted, and silently they walked their horses through the ribbons of mist that hung over the empty harvested fields of the fertile Medway valley. As they neared their destination the great pile of Penshurst Place loomed densely black against the ghostly grey of the pre-dawn sky. Richard scrutinized the massive fortified manor house intently; there was not a glimmer of light nor any sign of life. He wondered whether the man who now rested behind those thick walls would still prove to be his loyal kinsman when this day was done or would he, as Francis was convinced, turn out to be up to his neck in treachery. Sir James Tyrell, who had been sent ahead by Richard with a company of men at arms, stepped out from beneath the arched entrance of the squat turreted gatehouse and saluted his king silently. "Were you successful?" Richard questioned in a low voice, leading his mount through the raised portcullis.

"Aye, sire...I planted some of your men on the inside without raising any suspicions." He gave the king a sly sidelong look and grinned. "After dark, when the time was right, they quietly divested the guards of their livery and slipped into their places."

"No one was harmed?" the king demanded sharply.

The burly knight's prominent brown eyes surveyed him calmly. Having been in Richard's service for many years, he was well used to his master's concern for the welfare of the blameless folk who became embroiled in the intrigues of their overlords. The hardened soldier shook his head briefly. "Don't fret yourself, my liege, none of them suffered anything more than a sore head. They are now safely under guard in the cellars. Clad only in their shirts and braies, they will find it somewhat chilly down there but a little discomfort will not harm them." His smile turned into low rumbling laughter as he continued to relate his recent clandestine activities. "Two of my young squires turned themselves into scullions and insinuated themselves into the kitchen and buttery. They used the poppy juice provided by your apothecary judiciously – by the end of supper time many of the duke's household were uncommonly tired... most are now slumbering contentedly in the arms of Morpheus. Rest assured, sire, your visit here will remain secret, only my men and those accompanying you here this night, all of whom would die before betraying you, will ever know of it...apart from the duke of course," the knight muttered darkly.

Observing the look of withering contempt contorting Sir James's homely features, Richard realized that Francis had not been alone in harbouring doubts about Henry. Beside him his horse shifted restlessly, the noise of its hooves striking the cobbles echoed loudly around the courtyard. It was time to make a move. Hurriedly Richard handed over the reins to a waiting man at arms. "You did well, James...are all abed now?"

The knight nodded. "Aye, sire...most are, except the Duke, his steward and his body squire... these two are at the duke's constant beck and call ...I let them go about their usual duties so he would not suspect anything was amiss." Sir James's eyes gleamed mischievously. "It only took a little persuasion on my part to get their agreement to act as if nothing untoward had taken place here." He stopped and thought for a moment. "One more thing you should know, my lord...a courier arrived from Brecknock castle just before sunset with a bulky satchel for the duke. After demanding a flagon of wine he gave orders that he was not to be disturbed and shut himself in his document room...he remains there still."

The jingle of spurs and tramp of their heavy leather boots resounded off the high hammer-beamed ceiling and thick walls of the vast banqueting hall as they followed Buckingham's steward down its length. At the foot of the stairway leading to the solar, Francis reached forward and pulled the terrified servant back; his fingers dug into his shoulder. "Remember...announce only the arrival of Viscount Lovell," he growled menacingly.

The man swallowed rapidly, his eyes darted nervously to the stern, silent man standing beside the viscount taking in the aura of power and authority that emanated from his spare frame. Nodding his head frantically the steward spun on his heel and hurriedly stumbled and tripped his way upwards. Rapping sharply on the closed door of the document room, he pushed it open without waiting for a response from within. "My lord..." the servant stood stiffly in the entrance, "the Viscount Lovell is below...he demands to see you immediately," he announced in a voice fractured by apprehension. Then as if anticipating the duke's refusal to see the visitor, he quickly added, "The viscount is accompanied by a large company of men-at-arms, your grace."

The duke of Buckingham made no acknowledgment of his presence when Francis stepped into the room. He continued to lean over the lengthy document spread out on the table in front of him, his lips moving silently as he laboriously read the closely written lines. On reaching the end he rolled it up and tied a length of fabric around it. Laying it aside Henry Stafford raised black eyes filled with cold dislike to the man who stood by the door. "What brings Richard's dog sniffing into Kent?" he sneered with sly insolence.

The insulting allusion to the filthy rhyme penned by that seditious traitor Colyngbourne, who had counselled Henry Tudor on the best time and place for an invasion and conspired with the French king to give him assistance, had Francis clenching his teeth in anger. The temptation to draw his sword was intense; his hand hovered over the hilt of the blade hanging at his side. Overcoming his desire to skewer Buckingham, he bared his teeth in a snarl. "Have a care, Stafford... that the sharp fangs of the Lovell wolf do not tear you limb from limb," he threatened in a soft but deadly voice. Seeing the rage that blazed in the viscount's eyes, Buckingham saw that he had taken his antagonism for the king's closest friend a step too far. He quickly raised his hands in a gesture of appeasement. "Peace, my lord Lovell..." he said placatingly, "you and I have no love for one another but we are allies in our loyalty to the king and our concern for his well-being...come, state your business with me."

Before they began their urgent ride through the dark Kent countryside towards Penshurst Place, Francis and Richard had agreed upon the way to tackle Buckingham about the boys' disappearance. Francis was to sound Henry out before revealing anything himself but now, facing the duke's barely veiled hostility, he decided that a subtle approach would not work. The viscount opted for a direct attack. With contempt curling his lips he stalked across the room and stood directly in front of him. Watching Buckingham closely, he stated bluntly, "The king's nephews were abducted from the Tower eight nights ago... it was thought their mother had taken them but when the king confronted her she wept piteously and begged him to find them." Making no attempt to hide his conviction that Buckingham was involved, he demanded curtly, "What know you of this?"

Francis waited for the duke's explosion of outrage at being confronted with such obvious suspicion but to his surprise it did not come. Buckingham straightened and calmly walked out from behind the table, his broad, expressionless face gave nothing away. "Why do you come to me, Lovell?" he asked with unruffled self-possession. "After all, Brackenbury has total command at the Tower and sole charge of the bastards... no one gets past his guards... only he holds the keys to their rooms and has direct access to them." Switching to taunting, the duke continued softly, "How can I be responsible? I cannot walk through walls and locked doors."

Francis searched his face; the hard glitter behind Buckingham's eyes did nothing to allay his suspicions. He shook his head derisively. "By the Rood! You take me for a fool, Buckingham!" His voice was sharp with disbelief. "You as well as I know that as High Constable of England you have absolute authority over all but the king himself." The viscount's lips twisted into a sneering smile. "Shall I tell you how 'twas done?" The duke's mouth tightened but he made no response. Francis thought for a moment. "You will have intimidated some lowly guard commander and countermanded Brackenbury's orders. Having secreted your men somewhere in the Tower until you were ready to make your move, you set about purloining the keys, first ensuring that Sir Robert did not miss them. Spiriting the boys away, in the dead of night from under his very nose, would then have been a relatively simple undertaking." The viscount waited, unyielding determination written in every line of his grim countenance. Buckingham remained mute. "How close am I in my supposition, Buckingham?" Francis prodded mockingly.

A brooding silence filled the room, the air seethed with the antipathy that existed between the two men. At length the viscount let out an audible sigh. "Come, sir...tell me where the boys are?" He spoke with quiet forcefulness. "You have just pointed out that no outsiders can penetrate far enough into the Tower to take them...we are both aware of recent failed attempts to do so." He paused and gave the duke a long considering look. "Since leaving Richard at Gloucester, ostensibly to attend to urgent family matters, you have constantly been on the move ...the royal couriers have chased you from place to place." Francis continued to survey Buckingham, pinning him with his penetrating gaze. "It was as if you were trying to outrun them... stay beyond the king's reach... a closer inquiry into your activities has uncovered clandestine visits to London... you made one only days before the boys disappeared ... and departed just as stealthily after the alarm was raised in the Tower. Unluckily for you I had men stationed on all the routes in and out of the city. We caught up with you just outside Southwark on the Canterbury road. Such odd, furtive behaviour makes me extremely uneasy." The viscount's expression hardened. "Why the frequent hasty journeying...why the secrecy..."His expression darkened. "Are you plotting treason, Buckingham?" he demanded bluntly. Tilting his head slightly, Francis waited for some reaction from the duke.

At first Henry Stafford stared stoically back with guarded animosity but under the viscount's unwavering scrutiny his resolution began to waver. A slow flush stole over his swarthy features and his eyes slid away. The muscles in his heavy jaw flexed, his brows pulled together in a deep frown. The duke's mouth opened as if he intended to speak but then it closed abruptly and he pressed the tips of his blunt fingers to his lips. He drew in a long shuddering breath and rubbed a large hand repeatedly over his chin. His arrogant assurance slowly began to ebb away; uncertainty played over his face. Francis held still, scarcely daring to breathe while he watched Buckingham wrestle with indecision. *Would he speak? What would he reveal if he did?*

Making a strange hoarse sound, the duke suddenly spun away from the viscount. With agitated strides he paced to and fro and began speaking quietly, almost to himself. "For days I have been thinking on the best way to approach the king with this..." He hesitated..."with this news..." Breaking off, Buckingham came to an abrupt halt in front of the viscount. Thrusting his head forward, he scowled intently into Francis' face. "Perchance your unwelcome arrival here is a blessing after all," he muttered. Nodding to himself in affirmation of this idea he continued, "It is better coming from you who are closest to him." Having made up his mind to speak Buckingham's tone took on a sharper edge; his words became hurried and disjointed. "They were focuses for conspiracy and would have become ever more dangerous as they grew older ...progress from being pawns to plotters...packing them off to Flanders was not the answer... their very existence threatened Richard's position... he was not secure on the throne... they had to be eliminated... he being too tender hearted ...the task fell to others to..." His voice trailed away; turning back he stared over Francis' shoulder into the distance. "I did what had to be done..." A deathly silence followed his words; it was as if the stillness of the grave itself had descended upon the room.

Chapter 14

Just beyond the open door, Richard listened with an increasing sense of foreboding. His cousin's words made his blood run cold. A terrible fear began to grow in his chest. His heart started hammering, his whole body stiffened in rejection of what he was hearing. Shaking his head violently as if trying to dislodge the horror that was filling his mind, Richard stepped through the doorway. "In the name of God, Henry...say you have not harmed my nephews!" he demanded in a voice made hoarse by the ghastly dread that was running through him. Buckingham's head snapped round, their eyes locked and in his cousin's unblinking obsidian stare he read the fate of his brother's sons. Richard's face paled, taking on the grey hue of the room's cold stone walls; he shivered as icy sweat rolled down his spine. He gave an agonised whisper, "Sweet Jesu, they were nought but defenceless boys."

The duke trod towards him with heavy, purposeful strides, a fixed, intent look on his face. "The safety of England and the crown was jeopardized by the continued existence of your brother's bastard sons," he stated emphatically. "I was not alone in thinking this... you were not safe while they lived... it was done out of loyalty...I did what I thought was best... for you, Richard." Then a conspiratorial smile played over his lips and he leant forward. "After all...'tis only what you secretly wished for, sire," he added softly.

For a moment Richard was paralyzed by Henry's blatant attempt to link him to this hideous act. Repulsion raced through every nerve, artery and muscle in his body. He staggered slightly, horror sapping the strength from his legs. An all-consuming anger began to boil in him; outrage erupted into violent action. Richard delivered a back-handed blow across Buckingham's face, the force of which rocked the duke back on his heels. Raw fury glittered in his eyes. "God damn you to hell!" he cursed his cousin in a shaking voice. "You are mad...deranged...! Have taken leave of your senses! How can you think I desired something as vile, sinful and dishonourable as the murder of my nephews?" Grabbing a fistful of Henry's doublet Richard dragged him closer until they stood chest to chest. "That I would wish to have their blood on my hands!" He spat the words into his cousin's face. "And be damned for all eternity!" Pushing him violently away, Richard stood motionless, a frozen statue in the centre of the room whilst he fought the urge to attack Buckingham once more. At length a shudder ran through his rigidly held frame. Raising a trembling hand, he rubbed it back and forth over his eyes as if trying to wipe away the nightmare images of this cold-blooded murder of two innocent children from his mind. Finally, he straightened his shoulders and swung round to face the silent figure of the viscount who had become transfixed by Buckingham's hideous revelation. "Find Tyrrell!" Richard barked the order at his friend. "Now, Francis! Tell him to bring an escort..."

"Would that my brother's progeny were only daughters, if 'twas so King Richard's reign would be untroubled by challenge and strife." The words were spoken in a barely audible whisper but they hit Richard with the force of a battering ram. He gave a short gasp as shock drove the breath out of his body. Slowly he turned to face his cousin. Henry stared back at him, his eyes gleaming with a fanatical light. Wiping the blood from his damaged mouth the duke spoke softly, "Your wish has been granted cousin...Edward is survived only by daughters."

Richard's skin prickled with revulsion. He had spoken those words to his mother only hours after he had been crowned, when he had still been filled with self-doubt and apprehension for what the future held. Buckingham must have heard him and twisted his anxious musings into a desire for the boys' death. Bitter bile rose in his mouth as the hideous realization, that he was indirectly guilty of the murder of his nephews, seared into his brain. Self-loathing engulfed him. With those thoughtlessly spoken words he had prompted the death of two innocent boys. He felt himself drowning in a sea of black despair. A voice in the back of his mind repeatedly cried...Murderer! Waves of crushing agony pounded into his skull. He wanted to sink to his knees, howl his sorrow and remorse to the heavens and beg for forgiveness. As Richard's mind grappled with the nightmare of dealing with this hideous act and the man who had committed it in his name, he heard the viscount curse in a rough low voice, "By God! You will face justice for this act of madness, Buckingham...the king's intention was always to keep those boys safe and protected...he wished no harm to come to them!"

Buckingham stiffened. Looking directly at Richard he retorted in a coldly unrepentant tone, "Should you attempt to arrest and try me, I will proclaim long and loud that I acted on the king's orders."

The viscount snorted in disgust. "So much for your declaration that this accursed deed was a selfless action on your part, carried out for the good of the king and the country. I will stand witness against you...swear that you committed this foul, unholy act without the king's knowledge!" he snapped.

"...And who would believe the king's cur was not also involved?" the duke sneered scornfully. He was silent for a moment and then added, "My sealed confession is in the possession of someone in whom I have absolute trust...to be opened only if I am imprisoned on some false charge or meet my death in a violent or untimely manner." His black gaze swung back to the motionless king and his manner became more conciliatory. "We..." He coughed; clearing his throat, he continued, "I acted only in your best interests, sire... I have ever been your loyal servant... as long as I remain unharmed and at liberty you have nothing to fear from me."

The implicit threat behind these words and Henry's presumption in trying to control him, transformed Richard's despair into a savage burning anger. Seeing the king's face darken with fury and loathing, the duke's bravado leached away. A cajoling note entered his voice. "Be assured, cousin, 'twas done only to safeguard the throne of England."

Richard remained silent, all his suspicions on the alert. *Safeguard the throne for whom?* The question raced through his brain. If the boys' murder could be laid at his door and he and his son were eliminated, who stood to gain the most? Both Buckingham and Henry Tudor could claim to be heirs to the House of Lancaster but Buckingham's claim was the stronger. He had let slip that he was in league with others. All the suspicions voiced by Francis skittered around Richard's mind. Had that crafty churchman the Bishop of Ely worked on Henry, chiding him for supporting the Plantagenets, when his forebears had all been Lancastrian; reminded him that his father Humphrey had died fighting for them? Did his cousin believe he could take the throne for himself, or was he a pawn in the bishop's plan to put the Tudor on the throne? Richard's thoughts darted hither and thither. He finally concluded that Buckingham had not the guile to have acted alone...to plan the boys' murder and then use it against his king in an attempt to coerce and control him. Someone with far more cunning and foresight was guiding and counselling his unimaginative, avaricious cousin. Richard accepted at last the grim truth that Francis had been right all along. At some stage since his coronation, his cousin had decided that the enormous power and prestige he had been granted were no longer enough. Under the guise of kinship and loyalty Henry had begun working against him. An implacable desire for revenge uncoiled inside Richard but now, whilst rage, guilt and despair still held him in their grip, was not the time to act. Vengeance should be meted out coldly, with calculation. He knew what needed to be done. Firstly, he had to convince Henry that he understood and accepted that this abominable act had been carried out in his best interests. He would then watch and wait for Buckingham and his fellow conspirators to complete their traitorous plans and when they made their move he would be waiting – ready to strike.

They stood facing each other in the shadowy room. Richard watched his cousin impassively, his face set in an inscrutable mask. Under the king's cool surveillance, Buckingham shifted uneasily. With a faint smile hovering around his mouth, Richard watched the duke's growing discomfort for several moments then he turned and walked across the small chamber. He halted in front of a tall window overlooking the wide acres of parkland that stretched as far as the eye could see. His brooding gaze took in the first red traces of the sun rising in the eastern sky. A shiver of unease passed through him. How swiftly things changed: in the few short hours that lay between nightfall and daybreak his future and that of his family had become a murky uncertainty. He had intended his reign to be renowned for the justice, prosperity and peace it brought to all the people of England but already it was mired in murder and deceit. The boys had been under his protection. He could expect nothing but rumour, challenge and strife if he could give no satisfactory explanation for their disappearance. When he thought about the terrible predicament in which Buckingham had placed him, bitterness and rage rose once again to the surface, and he had to fight hard to control himself.

A tense silence stretched across the room. It wrapped a dark cocoon of anger, fear and guilt around the two men. Finally the king turned a face as composed and controlled as a marble effigy towards Buckingham. "I must accept that you took this action for my sake and for the safety of the throne." Richard was careful to keep his voice emotionless. "And because I understand that a few unthinking words spoken to my lady mother prompted you to this…" he faltered for a moment, "this deed … thinking 'twould please me, I feel that I cannot in all justification punish you…" The viscount's sharply indrawn breath and a faint hissing sound made through his clenched teeth signalled his friend's dismay and disapproval. Richard's eyes darted to his friend; he gave an almost imperceptible shake of his head then ignored him. There was time enough to explain himself to Francis after he had dealt with Buckingham. "…But neither will I reward you," he continued coldly. Buckingham glowered briefly at Francis then fixed his prominent eyes on the king and listened intently. "Therefore you will be escorted back to Brecknock Castle…"

The duke's face flushed with anger; he made a sharp negative motion with his head. "God's teeth!" he exploded fiercely. "You would arrest me..! Humiliate me…take me back as a prisoner to..!"

Richard's raised hand cut off his angry tirade. "You are not under arrest but you *will* stay in Wales, Henry…" he ordered emphatically. "You will stay away from the Court until I decide how to solve this unholy dilemma… understand me, cousin, I will countenance no disobedience in this instance…you will remain there until I summon you back." His hands fisting with impotent rage at what he perceived was the prospect of a public humiliation, Buckingham stood rigidly motionless and stared belligerently back at the king but he had sense enough to hold his tongue. Then, giving a curt bow, he turned abruptly on his heel and marched towards the door.

"Stop!" Richard's hard command sliced through the air halting the duke mid-stride. Coming up behind him the king's hand landed heavily on his shoulder; his merciless grip tightened until pain turned to numbness. "You will tell me now what you have done with my nephews and where their bodies lie," Richard demanded with quiet menace. Next morning the duke left Penshurst Place and returned to Wales. Richard never spoke to his cousin again.

Chapter 15

The gales of October had blown away the last remnants of summer when Buckingham and his nest of traitors raised their flag of rebellion in Kent and the West Country. It came as no surprise to Richard; he knew it was coming. Through his network of spies and men loyal to him, he had methodically harvested the details of their plan to depose and kill him and as Francis had foreseen, the Bishop of Ely was up to his neck in the plotting. He and Lady Stanley had secretly been fomenting rebellion for months. They were the brains behind this insurrection and vain, gullible Buckingham was their dupe, the instrument with which they intended to destroy Richard. They had seduced him into joining their conspiracy by feeding Henry's sense of self-importance and lust for power, convincing him that his Stafford bloodline had a more legitimate right to the crown than Richard and his nephews, but all the while they were playing a double game. It was clear that they had no intention of allowing Henry to gain the crown. Through their shared physician, Doctor Lewis Caerlon, who acted as go-between, Margaret Stanley and Elizabeth Woodville were planning for

Margaret's son's marriage to Elizabeth's eldest daughter.

The more he thought about Lady Stanley's actions, the more Richard was convinced that she had induced Buckingham to murder the boys. Her reason to wish them dead was compelling. If he was defeated and killed, with them already out of the way, the path was clear for her son to claim the crown as the accepted Lancastrian heir. His marriage to their sister, who would effectively be Edward's heir, cleverly forestalled all other claims to the throne, but having declared his intention to marry her, Henry Tudor would have to re-legitimise Elizabeth and her siblings; a queen could not be a bastard. Such a reinstatement gave the boys a prior claim to the throne. They therefore had to be disposed of, if she and Morton were to succeed with their diabolical plan.

When his spies reported that the bishop had been allowed to escape from Brecknock Castle Richard knew the traitors had begun to make their move; he was ready for them. His men tracked Ely across England. In the humble disguise of a friar, the wily cleric made his way into Kent and the home of Elizabeth Woodville's brother Earl Rivers. There his poisonous tongue whispered to the discontented Woodville and Lancastrian factions of the death of the princes by Richard's hand. The purpose of his wicked lies was to incite them into uniting and marching on London. They were to be the diversion that drew Richard there to defend the city. This would then allow Buckingham and his Welsh army to cross the Severn unopposed to link up with Henry Tudor and his Breton mercenaries, who were landing on the Devon coast. The plan was then to march on London, recruiting men with French gold, and having grown

133

in numbers and strength they would catch Richard unawares and destroy him – but he was already one step ahead of them.

As soon as he received the news that the Kent rebels were mustering, Richard raised his standard in Leicester. His spirits soared when he saw how men flocked to serve him. The common people trusted and accepted him as their rightful king, as did the great nobles of the realm, who remained staunchly loyal and to a man turned out to defend him. Along the Welsh border his supporters were already destroying the bridges over the Severn. In London, his cousin and faithful friend, John Howard was waiting with his troops for the Kentish rebels to attack. After sending its citizens a warm message of encouragement – bidding them to have faith in their stout walls and in the military prowess of the duke of Norfolk – Richard marched westwards to confront the men who sought to wrest his kingdom from him.

It was then that the heavens affirmed that he was indeed England's rightful king by unleashing violent tempests all over country. Torrents of cold sleeting rain poured down day after day. The roads turned into muddy mires and became impassable. The great river Severn rose relentlessly until it finally burst its banks. The floods spread for miles, drowning man and beast. The sodden Kent rebels quickly lost their enthusiasm for war and returned to the dry warmth of their hearths. The Duke of Buckingham became trapped in Wales; having no love for their brutal, hard-dealing overlord, his half- drowned, reluctant Welsh army deserted him en masse. Seeing their treacherous enterprise crumble and collapse around them, his cousin's mentors were also swift to abandon their puppet to his fate. The bishop fled into the Fens and Lady Stanley sought sanctuary with her husband. In the turbulent waters of the Channel, Henry Tudor's ships were tossed and scattered by the storms. His bedraggled fleet limped into Plymouth to find no rebel army waiting to hail him as king. With his ambitions in tatters, the pretender turned his ships around and slunk back to Brittany. Richard's enemies had exposed themselves as traitors for all to see and the great betrayer was himself betrayed.

The prisoner raised red-rimmed bloodshot eyes alight with anticipation when the hinges of the heavy cellar door creaked and it was pushed open. The lantern held aloft by his visitor cast dim rays of light into the damp, airless chamber, slowly pushing back the thick, gloomy darkness that pervaded every corner. Viscount Lovell shook his head and spoke in a low voice. "He will not see you. The false confession you are threatening him with has been found amongst the papers Ely left behind when he fled. There will be no trial; your guilt is plain for all to see. If you do not wish to meet your Maker unshriven 'tis best you summon a priest and make your confession this night... there will scarce be time on the morrow. The headsman has arrived... they are building the scaffold as I speak."

The fastidious Duke of Buckingham was a sorry sight to behold. Clad in the stained, woollen coat of a labourer, he was slumped on a low bench that was the only piece of furniture in the bare cellar room. Francis Lovell tried to find some compassion for the wretched figure in front of him but it was hard to feel any sympathy for his plight. This vain, greedy man was a threefold betrayer, without honour or conscience. He had done away with the king's nephews; from his frantic garbled excuses while under interrogation, it was still unclear whether it was done in anticipation of rich rewards from Richard or to gain the crown for himself – it no longer mattered. What was a certainty was his embroilment in Ely's conspiracy to put Henry Tudor on the throne and now that that had failed, thinking to save his own skin, he had shamelessly betrayed his fellow conspirators and disclosed every sordid detail of their plotting.

"There will be no reprieve, Buckingham, the king will have no change of heart, your betrayal burned deeply…you will face the axe before noon tomorrow."

Henry Stafford ground his teeth in frustration; he had pinned his hopes on being able to use that confession to bargain himself to freedom. He stood up stiffly; the shackles and chains around his wrists and ankles rattled and clinked against each other. As he watched the once all-powerful duke get laboriously to his feet, the thought ran through Francis' mind '*how the mighty have fallen*'. "Richard quickly forgets that I made him king," Buckingham snarled viciously, kicking out at the tankard and plate containing the congealed remains of his recent meal. "It was my words that persuaded the Council and Parliament to petition him to accept the crown."

The viscount's mouth set into a grim line of distaste at the duke's self-delusion; of his likening himself to Richard Neville, the powerful earl of Warwick. Then the thought passed through Francis' mind that they did share one characteristic – an overweening ambition for power. "And it was not enough that he put his complete trust in you; raised you to be second only to him in rank and power. Your self-serving vanity demanded more so you plotted with his enemies to destroy him!" the viscount responded acidly, shaking his head in disgust. "You are the creator of your own downfall, Buckingham…be grateful that the king has been merciful and spared you the ignominy of a traitor's death by hanging, drawing and quartering." Placing the lantern down on the rough earthen floor to give the condemned man some light during his last hours, Francis turned to leave the room. He looked back over his shoulder as the guard pulled the door closed. "It is only your noble rank that is saving you from it."

The small crowd assembled around the makeshift scaffold, which had hastily been erected on Salisbury's market square, shivered in the raw November air. Word had rapidly spread around the city that the execution of that great traitor the Duke of Buckingham, who had been handed over to the Sherriff of Shrewsbury by one of his own servants, was about to take place. A few in the gathering grumbled that this event was hardly worth turning out for on this freezing Sunday morning as there would be little entertainment for 'twas to be a mere beheading and not a proper traitor's execution. Suddenly all eyes shifted to the doorway of the Blue Boar Inn through which the prisoner, manacled and sullen, was being led. The guards steered him towards the scaffold where the block sat centre stage. The duke stood on the gallows, with disbelief etched in every line of his broad features. He gazed haughtily around and then down into the crowd. His expression stalled when his eyes took in the headsman, patiently leaning on the long handle of his axe at the foot of the scaffold. It was then that the harsh reality of his imminent death struck home. His aloof demeanour suddenly underwent a dramatic change. He began to fight wildly against the chains that bound his hands behind his back and in a high, shrill, desperate voice he demanded audience with the king for he had vitally important information that his highness would be keen to know. Swiftly the executioner mounted the scaffold. He made short work of blindfolding the struggling duke and pushed him to his knees. Buckingham's bound hands flailed uncontrollably; repeatedly his body reared away from the block until his head was finally forced down. The onlookers began jeering and stamping their feet, demanding the traitor show some courage like a true nobleman and give them a good death. The headsman's first blow severed Buckingham's arm; his piercing, animal-like scream of agony silenced them momentarily. The second blow was true and the traitor's head toppled into the straw. Making their way along Blue Boar Row, many in the dispersing crowd shook their heads and muttered scornfully of the duke's cowardly, ignoble end.

As the first clod of earth was being turned for his grave in the Inn's yard, two figures in long hooded cloaks emerged from beneath the shadowy arches of the Poultry Cross. Making their way across the cobbles, they came to a halt beside the scaffold. The slighter figure leant forward; gently toeing Buckingham's bloody corpse with his booted foot, he murmured, "For shame, Henry Stafford, you betrayed your king and dishonoured your royal bloodline, but ultimately you betrayed yourself for in the end you were without integrity, dignity or courage."

Richard watched the monks gently lower the coffins containing his nephews' earthly remains into the small vault adjoining his brother's burial chamber. After Buckingham had revealed their whereabouts, he and Francis had found them deep in the chilly bowels of St Thomas's Tower. Wrapped in a thick tapestry, their young bodies had been hidden in an ancient iron bound chest along with the feather pillows that had suffocated them. His mind went back to the moment they had found the boys. "What now, Dickon?" Francis had asked sadly as they gazed down into their pallid, waxy faces whose wide sightless eyes would forever haunt him. "Do you announce them dead?"

With guilt and remorse eating into him, Richard sank to his knees and began to pray soundlessly. At length he rose to his feet. "Would that I could, Francis, but who will believe that I did not order them dead...and if I remain silent...? How long before my cousin breaks his word?" he asked in a flat voice. A bleak smile crossed his face "I am damned if I do and damned if I don't."

The viscount frowned and stepped closer to the king. "There must be an answer to this dilemma, Dickon?" A small sardonic laugh erupted from Richard. "If there is...I have not yet found it, my friend." He paused and then in a decisive voice continued, "But until I do and until I have dealt with Buckingham and his plotters, I will leave my nephews in the care of my trusted Grey Friars."

The solemn chanting by the monks of prayers from The Offices of the Dead brought Richard back to the present. He looked down at his brother's coffin. It was still draped with his royal standard and surrounded by the staves of office that his Councillors had thrown into their dead master's tomb as his body was lowered into the vault. He recalled how his right to be chief mourner at his brother's funeral had been denied him by Elizabeth Woodville and her cronies; they had buried Edward without even letting him know that he was dead. The murder of these two innocents was a direct result of the chaotic aftermath of his death. At least in death the sons would be reunited with the father; the infant George* and young Mary*, for whom Edward had built the adjoining vault, would not begrudge resting a while longer in the Quire so that their brothers could lie close to their father. In the flickering torch-light the long shadow that hovered over his brother's coffin wavered then shifted to the two smaller coffins of his sons. Richard gave a convulsive shiver. Had the uneasy spirit of his brother come to join in this sad secret burial? His mind reached out to Edward. *If only you had not allowed your lust for Elizabeth Woodville to rule you, brother...I would now be the protector and loyal subject of your legitimate heirs and the kingdom would not be in danger of yet again being torn apart by war.'* Richard drew in a long painful breath. *'The hand of our cousin killed your sons, Edward but Lady Stanley willed the deed. Buckingham has paid for his crimes and I have her cornered. Sadly, her partner in crime, the Bishop of Ely, has escaped to Flanders where he will without a doubt continue plotting against our family but he will not succeed. I will vanquish these murderous Lancastrians once and for all and then the world shall know the truth behind this monstrous crime.'*

Chapter 16

Eden 2015

Atonement! Richard started. The word raced through his mind as he returned to an awareness of his present surroundings. He could tell from the soft pearly light in the room that dawn was breaking. Entirely caught up in the past he had remained motionless in front of the cold hearth throughout the long hours of the night. Pushing himself upright he wearily flexed his shoulders and tried to stretch out the cramped muscles along his spine. Walking the length of the book-lined chamber to the tall mullioned windows at the far end, he stood and watched the snow-covered mountain peaks guarding this holy valley of Eden turn a luminescent pink as the sun ascended high into the heavens above them. Closing his eyes, he leant his aching brow against the thick cool glass; the knuckles of both hands pressed down hard against the unyielding stone sill. Once he had expiated his sins to the satisfaction of divine justice, he had resolutely not allowed himself to revisit the past but now he could not stop the memories from flooding into his brain. Buckingham had paid for his crimes with his life and Parliament had passed a bill of attainder for high treason against that most devious and wicked of women, Margaret Stanley. Many of his Councillors had pushed for her to receive the same punishment as Buckingham but it was not the Plantagenet way to behead women, no matter how treacherous. His mouth twisted with distaste – that practice he had left to the vicious Tudors.

He had taken the crown and set aside Edward's sons to save the realm from civil war and his family from being destroyed by the scheming of another evil woman. One of his first actions as king had been to rid the kingdom of the sin and tyranny that his brother's reign had descended into under Elizabeth Woodville's malign influence. To free the country from the corrupt grip of her family and acolytes he had passed laws that protected the innocent and gave all his people the right to fair and impartial justice.* A faint ironic smile crossed Richard's face; laws which still guided the legal system of England to this day. Peace and order were restored; the country was content under his rule and then Buckingham's foul deed blighted everything he had striven to achieve. The conviction that he was guilty by association of the boys' murder took hold of his mind and gave him no peace; it tormented him and gnawed into his soul. Sleep became an elusive stranger and when he did slide into an exhausted slumber his dreams were filled with nightmare visions of their dead accusing eyes. The burden of it became intolerable.

Richard recalled his desperate attempt to make peace with God whilst visiting Sandwich to inspect the port's fortifications against the French. One evening as soon as darkness descended, he and Francis slipped quietly out of the town to meet the viscount's kinsman Thomas Lovell who was waiting with a small escort of trusted men at arms to escort them to Hall Place, Thomas's home near the village of Harbledown. There he donned the sclavein, mantelet and wide-brimmed hat of a pilgrim and in this humble anonymous guise he joined the constant stream of penitents who walked barefoot along the pilgrim's route to Canterbury. In the cathedral, he prostrated himself in front of Becket's shrine and prayed fervently to the saint to intercede for him. The damp chill that rose up from the tiled floor, leached deeply into his bones, making his body quake and shiver violently. He lay there until the break of day but found no absolution.

When the unspeakable happened and his beloved ten-year-old son had died suddenly at Easter, almost a year to the day of his brother's death, and his adored Anne was taken from him a few short months later, he became certain that he was being dealt divine retribution. He and Anne were holding Court in Nottingham's great fortress castle when they were brought the terrible news of Edward's sudden death. Almost insane with shock and grief they rushed back to Middleham to be met by young Edward's distraught governess who voiced her suspicion that he had been poisoned. Richard's blood ran cold on hearing Mistress Idley's frenzied sobbing. "He was well, sire!" she insisted brokenly. "I do swear upon my soul! There was nary a sign of sickness when I settled the sweetling for the night! The prince was full of high spirits and childish joy at the prospect of joining you and the queen at Nottingham. He was too excited to drink his honeyed milk, so I set the cup down on the coffer beside his bed where he could reach for it should he become thirsty in the night... it was in the early hours of the morning that he fell violently ill, first he began to sweat then to shiver... and then the terrible pains in his belly began." Her face twisted in anguish at her remembered helplessness. "Nothing I did helped…" her voice rose, "not warm poultices…not the fennel and mint syrup I had him swallow…" She rubbed a trembling hand across her tear-reddened eyes. Smothering a sob she turned a bleak sorrow-filled face to Richard and choked out, "He had drunk all the milk from the cup I left beside his bed…" Her voice trailed away, her words hung ominously in the air. With a despairing wail she buried her face in her hands and wept inconsolably.

With eyes showing the tortured dullness of disbelief, Richard gazed back at the distraught woman. The small hairs at the nape of his neck began to prickle and he felt a terrible throat-constricting fear. Had the malevolence of the Bishop of Ely and Margaret Stanley reached Middleham? Had one of his own people betrayed him and poisoned Edward at their behest? Despite ransacking the castle and interrogating all his retainers he had never found any proof, but nevertheless the suspicion lingered forever in Richard's mind. They laid their sweet boy to rest in the church at Middleham. When the family mausoleum he planned to build in York Minster was completed, they would move him there.

Anne never recovered from the blow of Edward's death; soon she too began to sicken. The slight cough from which she intermittently suffered returned, only this time it steadily worsened, continually wracking her slender frame and painting her lips crimson with blood. The royal physicians tried all manner of remedies but he could only stand by and watch helplessly as day by day the woman whom he had loved for as long as he could remember, faded into a pale wraith and then quietly slipped away from him. At the hour of her death the sun, the symbol of the Plantagenets, darkened and day turned into night. After a few moments the sun's light did return but he never emerged from the shadowy world of sorrow that her death had plunged him into. He did not doubt then that these dreadful calamities were heaven's judgement of an 'eye for an eye' against him. How else could the timing of his son's death and the eclipse of the sun when Anne took her last breath be explained? He had taken the crown, not from a craving for power but out of duty, and by doing so he had set in motion a train of events that had cost him those whom he held most dear and culminated in his own violent death on the marshy plain of Redemore.

Richard pushed open the lattice pane; taking a deep steadying breath of the crisp early spring air into his lungs, he forced his mind back to those last weeks before his final battle. He recalled how news of Henry Tudor's imminent invasion came as a relief. His Court had become a hotbed of vicious rumour and speculation. Hiding in Antwerp, that master of betrayal, the Bishop of Ely had worked ceaselessly to discredit him and proclaim Henry Tudor's right to the throne. He had used the Church's wealth to bribe men to viciously vilify him. His gold fuelled a never-ending whispering campaign of monstrous lies; that he had ordered the killing of his nephews, had poisoned Anne, intended to incestuously marry his niece and even murdered his brother Clarence. The filthy falsehoods spread like the plague. Fleetingly Richard felt again the frustrated fury and sense of helplessness which consumed him when men began to look at him with questions in their eyes. His ways were those of a soldier, he valued and rewarded duty, loyalty and integrity. As a warrior he had fought his enemies openly and honourably, and treated those whom he defeated with respect. He had no weapons with which to fight against the evil web of lies and intrigue that Ely and Margaret Stanley spun around him. He had publicly denounced and refuted the despicable rumours to an assembly of Lords at the Hospital of St John but the poisonous words continued to circulate. Wearied to the bone by the divisions and tensions surrounding him, heartsick and grieving for his lost loved ones, Richard remembered thinking *'heaven has taken my wife and son from me in retribution for my grievous error but I am England's rightful king...I will not allow Henry Tudor to take my throne,'* as he had marched out from Leicester towards his rendezvous with destiny. On the battlefield he learnt the bitter truth that it mattered not whether right was on his side – justice could not prevail against the treachery and betrayal of base men. Of its own volition his hand moved up to massage the back of his head as if to soothe away the memory of vicious pain. His expression stilled, growing grim as the ironic thought flashed through his brain that the halberd and axe may have dealt the blows but Ely's venomous words had already destroyed him long before the battle took place and Thomas Stanley's men brought him down in the marsh.

He had atoned for his sins in the divine crucible of Purgatory but his feeling of guilt over the murder of his nephews never left him. He had resisted ascending into the realm of the blessed for so long because he still felt himself to be unworthy. He did not believe that a soul with a reputation besmirched and stained, with a name that was a watchword for evil, should reside among pure and unblemished souls. And then there was the question that had haunted him since he had come to understand what the reality of Purgatory was. Would he, Anne and young Edward be reunited once they each had travelled their own path of atonement? Fearing the answer, he had lacked the courage to ask Gilbert. As long as he didn't know he could hope.

Caught up in his introspective musing Richard failed to register Gilbert's quiet entry into the library until he felt the monk's calm presence at his side. The two men stood gazing out over the sacred valley, each preoccupied with his own thoughts, until Gilbert's grave voice broke the silence between them. "Forgive yourself and shed your feelings of guilt and shame, Dickon," the monk commanded sternly. "You have long been free from any stain of sin, and by clinging to them you do yourself a great disservice. There was neither malice nor intent behind the words you spoke to your mother. You did not wish for the death of your brother's sons...the crime was committed by the Duke of Buckingham whose hand was guided by others...not you!" he insisted forcefully. Father Gilbert watched Richard closely. His friend's chiselled features could not hide the intense emotions battling for supremacy inside him – remorse, shame, doubt and hope all swept across his expressive face. The monk pressed home his point. "And you would do well to remember that it is impossible for the human heart to hide from divine scrutiny. The truly evil are never granted redemption; yet here you are in Eden – heaven's waiting room...your self-hatred has no place here, Dickon, let go of it...it is a slight on heaven's judgement," the monk stressed emphatically.

Without acknowledging the priest's words, Richard continued to stare into the distance. Slowly acceptance eased the lines of strain from his face but Father Gilbert saw that something still disturbed him and waited. At length, he turned a sombre face to his mentor. "And yet I will eternally be known as the infamous child-killer king." A wistful note entered his voice. "A selfish wish I know but I had thought to be rid of that foul stain on my name before I departed from here." He paused, dropping his head. He rubbed the tight muscles at the back of his neck and gave a hollow, self-deprecating chuckle. "But then the victor has always written history and Will Shakespeare, that greatest of all wordsmiths, took the Tudors at their word...sealing my reputation for all time," he murmured ruefully.

Anticipating that Father Gilbert had come to tell him that he must now leave this sanctuary, Richard drew himself up to his full height; his lean body took on the straight-backed stance of a knight about to do battle with the enemy. "I accept that I cannot linger here any longer, Gilbert and will abide by the decision of the Guardians." He hesitated a moment before raising a proud pale face to the monk, who took in the combination of pain and hope burning behind his intelligent eyes. In a low hoarse voice he demanded, "Tell me they will be waiting for me...my wife... my son."

Father Gilbert cleared his throat and swallowed hard. Compassion for this courageous soul rose up in him like a great wave; he was about to cause him yet further pain. Reaching forward, he put an arm around Richard's shoulders in a rough gesture of comfort. "My friend, this I cannot do." The monk searched his mind for an explanation that he would understand. "The Church teaches that heaven is like Elysium... a beautiful, glowing place full of sweet music, fragrant scents and light airy halls... a place full of love, where sin and the limitations and imperfections of the flesh have been cast off, and where there will be a happy reunion between loved ones, who will live a perfect life together forever." Father Gilbert paused, drew in a deep breath and then continued. "But this is not entirely true." His arm dropped away and he looked at Richard with eyes full of regret. "In reality once a soul is purified it passes into the Empyrean – where the angels and the blessed reside. There it is filled with light and knowledge...a reunion with loved ones as you understand it does not take place." Beside him Richard's body tensed. "I can give you the assurance that Anne and your son have long since entered the Empyrean... when you also take that final step, Dickon, you will at long last all be in that blessed place." The monk hesitated. "But whether your souls will ever meet in that vast celestial radiance I cannot say." Unable to bear the growing hopelessness he saw in his friend's face, he turned his gaze back out on to the gardens; there, a small robin, perched on the edge of a sundial, was holding a host of aggressive sparrows at bay. His throat tightened; the courage shown by the tiny outnumbered bird against such overwhelming odds, put him so much in mind of the man who stood beside him.

Richard's heart lurched; a cold knot formed in his stomach; the spark of hope that had sustained him through all his trials was finally snuffed out. It was hard enough knowing that he would forever be parted from his son but to be endlessly separated from his precious wife, the better half of him, without whom he was not whole...suddenly he couldn't breathe, despair ate into his brain, his legs threatened to buckle under him. Richard slumped against his mentor; momentarily he leant against the monk's broad frame for support while he gathered his strength. Pushing himself upright he turned and with the heavy tread of an old man he moved back to the huge fireplace. Dropping into one of the padded leather chairs flanking the hearth, Richard stared down into the cold fireplace and spoke in a hollow voice. "Knowing that they are there yet having no prospect of being reunited with my wife and son will make heaven a place of torment, not peace, for me." He shook his head despondently and with an almost imperceptible note of pleading in his voice, he turned towards the monk. "I accepted that a long separation from Anne and Edward was likely to be part of my penance but to lose them forever..." Richard's face twisted in anguish and he gave a bitter laugh. "Can a saved soul request relegation – to the purifying fires... they could burn away my memories and the desolation I feel now."

The defeatism behind these words shocked father Gilbert. "Have you lost your wits, Dickon?" the monk demanded in a harsh voice. "You will put such thoughts out of your mind and listen to me...I have not finished yet!" he ordered sharply. "The Guardians are adamant...you must leave."

Richard gave a resigned shrug of his shoulders. "To ascend into a vast, lonely unknown," he retorted dryly. "Why does it feel like a punishment, Gilbert?"

A warning frown crossed Father Gilbert's face; his mouth thinned with displeasure. "Do not question this decision, Richard; there is good reasoning behind it. You cannot stay here indefinitely. Without celestial light and divine sustenance your soul will eventually wither away and die. The next world is not what you have been taught to expect but in spite of what you think you *will* find peace and contentment there," the monk stressed emphatically. He strode rapidly down the length of the library and seated himself opposite his protégé. Their eyes met, and Richard's brows pulled together in a wary frown but he did not speak.

After a few moments of reflection Father Gilbert sat forward on the edge of his seat and continued. "There has been much discussion and debate among the Guardians about what is best for you, given your frame of mind – your unabating self-loathing that is preventing you from forgiving yourself and subconsciously rejects your soul's purity." He smiled faintly. "A rare but not unheard-of condition in Purgatory...and one that we have very little experience in dealing with," he muttered beneath his breath. He fixed his penetrating gaze on Richard and with a strange, unreadable expression on his face studied him intently. A prickle of apprehension rippled along Richard's spine. What solution had the Guardians come up with? "Some amongst us feel that you should make an immediate ascent to Heaven, believing that once you are there this irrational self-hatred will simply disappear. Others think this too drastic and that the remedy is for you to transmigrate – to live another mortal life... they believe the living of another life will weaken the grip that the past has on your mind and consequently the antipathy you harbour towards yourself," explained the monk. His words were greeted with an astonished silence. Leaning back into his chair Father Gilbert frowned and rubbed his jaw reflectively, as if he was not entirely sure about the wisdom of the decision that had been had reached. "We finally agreed that the decision should ultimately be yours – that you should be the master of your fate."

Richard was thunderstruck, rendered speechless with incredulity. He could scarcely believe what he was hearing. The Guardians were offering him an alternative to an immediate move into the Afterlife. Gilbert was talking about reincarnation! His head began to pound. Whichever choice he made the stark truth remained…he and Anne were forever lost to each other… knowing this, he had no burning desire to enter Paradise…but did he want another chance at a mortal life? Richard let the idea sink into his mind, reflecting that if he couldn't be with her then reincarnation and the prospect of lifting the burden of self-loathing that weighed so heavily on him was tempting… but there were so many questions that needed an answer before he could consider taking this enormous step; the foremost of which was: would he retain any memory of his previous life?

The urgent voice of his mentor interrupted his whirling thoughts. "You must understand, Dickon, that you will be born into the 21st century…a world vastly different from the world you inhabited when you were Richard of Gloucester and king of England." Richard stood up. Rolling the tension from his shoulders, he stepped towards the hearth; bracing himself over the mantle he kicked at the burnt-out logs in the fireplace and watched them crumble into ash. "But not unfamiliar to me, Gilbert," he reflected. "For centuries of earthly time I have been a fascinated observer of humanity, witnessing its enormous courage and compassion and its capacity for barbarism. I have watched the rise and fall of dynasties and ideologies; seen men conquer the oceans – sailing out from Europe in their flimsy wooden ships to discover new and fascinating continents and felt shame and sadness to see the peoples of these new worlds enslaved by their fellow man. I have watched men take to the skies and reach the moon…marvelled at the progress of medical knowledge – had Anne and Edward lived today modern medicine would have saved them. And I have despaired as humanity tore itself apart with war… inventing ever more sophisticated weapons with which to destroy itself…" Father Gilbert's gruff comment of "watching is vastly different from actual experience, Dickon," broke into Richard's flow of words. He turned towards the monk who returned his gaze with a speculative gleam in his eyes. Richard felt a curious ripple of anticipation course through him. "For you to make a reasoned and well-considered decision, we feel it necessary that you revisit the mortal world." A quiet humour coloured the monk's solemn tone; his lips curved in a faint reminiscent smile. "With me as your guide you will once again walk among the living."

Chapter 17

Filling his lungs with the damp, earthy air of an English wood in springtime, Richard rested a booted foot on the lowest rung of the post and rail fence over which he leant. It was good to be back. His fingers idly played with the budding twig he had plucked from an overhanging branch as he followed Gilbert's purposeful stride along the overgrown footpath that led them here; which petered out in the field beyond. From the surrounding landscape of rolling wooded hills and fertile farmland, he guessed they were somewhere in middle England. Absently snapping the stick into small pieces and letting them fall aimlessly to the moss covered ground Richard laughed to himself. Gilbert had certainly made sure that he had a thorough knowledge of what life in a 21st century world would entail. He had flown in aeroplanes, ridden on trains, driven in cars and become familiar with all the technological paraphernalia of modern life. He had visited military barracks, law courts, prisons, hospitals and Silicon Valley. The monk had walked him through the corridors of power of all the great nations where he had seen democracy and autocracy at work. He had taken him to the battlefields of the Middle East, to the poverty and want in Africa; and the refugee camps of the displaced. He had quickly learned that humanity had changed very little since he last walked the earth – it was still capable of great good and enormous evil. Richard had been fascinated by all that he had seen and experienced but still remained undecided about living in this advanced yet brutal world.

Richard turned towards his mentor who was leaning back against the fence, seemingly fascinated by a rosy breasted bullfinch calling mournfully for its mate from a branch above their heads. His relaxed stance belied the air of tension that surrounded him. The monk lowered his eyes briefly and Richard was captured again by that enigmatic, penetrating look that had been there when he had told him of the Guardians' decision. Saying nothing, Gilbert returned his attention to the bird but something was making him nervous and it had to do with their present surroundings. Clearly, Gilbert had brought him here for a reason although Richard was at a loss to understand what it was. His eyes ranged over the farmland that lay in front of him and he tried to find some clues but all he could see was a large meadow in which the ground rose up to and then fell away from a line of trees. Mystified, Richard examined it more closely. The grass grew lush and vibrant green. Small clusters of early Kingcups were turning bright yellow faces up to the sun and here and there he could see odd tufts of marsh grass being blown about by the cool breeze. A faint frown appeared between his eyes. It was unusual to see such grass growing in cultivated fields; it usually grew in swamps. As that thought crossed his mind he became aware of the damp sponginess of the ground beneath his feet. Richard's pondering stuttered to a halt...soft ground...marsh grass... kingcups... also known as marsh-mallow. The signs were all there, he was in all probability standing on a reclaimed marsh. His sharp mind snapped to attention...a drained swamp in the Midlands...was it too much of a coincidence? The word Redemore insinuated itself into his brain. For a second he rejected the idea and its implications until he recalled the feeling of familiarity that had assailed him when they walked along the old Roman road named Fen Lane to get to this wooded footpath. He had not attached any significance to it – England was crisscrossed by Roman roads – but he recalled that the road cut through a wide shallow valley. The marsh had gone. Copses of trees and the straight hedge lines of cultivated fields now enclosed what five hundred years ago had been a flat open plain but the overall terrain remained the same. He and his knights had made their ill-fated charge along that very road. Richard's flesh crawled, his stomach muscles knotted, he fought down the desire to retch. Dragging in deep breaths of air he turned a stony face towards the monk. "You saw a need to bring me back here?" he demanded. "To the place where I was betrayed, hacked to pieces and dishonour..." His voice cracked. For a moment he couldn't speak. Fighting to control his emotions he turned away and stared across the field. Visions of the past crowded into his mind. He saw again the carnage that took place on that fateful day and the gruesome images of his own violent death. Richard jerked himself back to the present. "In God's holy name tell me why you are tormenting me in this manner, Gilbert!" Pain and confusion laced his voice. "Why bring me here after all this time...is this some form of test...or a penalty?" he asked bitterly. "Do the Guardians wish me to relive the horror and degradation that was heaped upon me before they allow me to...?" The monk's powerful voice broke through his tirade. "Enough, Dickon! You shame them and yourself for thinking in such a way!"

Richard's narrowed eyes grimly searched the monk's face and tried to reach into his mind, without any success. "Then for pity's sake tell me why you have brought me here!" Richard's hoarse voice held the raw edge of all the horror he was remembering.

Gilbert looked calmly back at him. "You needed to revisit this place in order to understand what is yet to come," he stated cryptically. With a haunted expression Richard turned away. "You trusted me throughout all your trials and tests during your journey of atonement...did I ever let you down?" the monk demanded. A tense silence was the only response. Gilbert studied his friend's averted profile for a short while then sighed. "Trust me now, Dickon...it will not be misplaced," he said softly – almost pleadingly.

Hitching up the skirt of his habit, the monk climbed over the fence and made his way across the field. After a moment Richard followed him. Silently, they climbed the hill that overlooked it. As they crested the brow Richard immediately recognized the rudely simple church that stood in front of him. The weathered oak shingled bell-cote had been replaced by a squat red brick turret, and stucco now covered the half-timbered walls, but it was unmistakably Dadlington church. On the morning of the battle, in those darkest hours just before the break of dawn, restlessness had driven him up this same hill and he had found this humble ancient house of God. The solitary hour he had spent in prayer here had brought him a measure of peace and an acceptance of whatever fate awaited him.

Slowly they walked amongst the scattered mounds and stone monuments in the ancient churchyard. He did not need telling that the bones of his comrades-in-arms lay beneath his feet. The booming sound of canon fire resounding over the countryside broke their quiet contemplation. For an instant it transported Richard back in time – to the battle and then he remembered he was in the 21st century and that cannons had evolved into powerful mechanized artillery such as howitzers and mortars. The simple field cannon was now only used for ceremonial purposes. His gaze turned in the direction of the sound; the guns were being fired from the top of Ambion Hill where he had deployed some of his troops to prevent that high ground from being taken by the rebels. He counted twenty-one rounds. "A royal salute," Gilbert murmured, coming to stand beside him. With a bleak smile Richard turned on his heel and began to thread his way through the gravestones towards the gate. Any salute fired around here could only be to honour his victorious adversary he decided. He failed to see an azure and crimson banner, bearing his white boar device, unfurl itself from a tall flagpole in a sudden gust of wind and flutter high above the hill. With a thoughtful expression, Father Gilbert stood and watched the long swallow-tailed pennant flap and then stream out over the plain. After a while he squared his broad shoulders and went to find his protégé.

In Sutton Cheyney the iron bands that had wrapped themselves around his chest at the battle site, loosened a little when Richard came across a memorial to himself and those who had fought for his cause. There mounted on the wall in a prominent place in the nave of the church, was a large brass plaque flanked by two embroidered banners. On one side was his royal standard and on the other his personal emblem. On the stone shelf below it lay a fresh wreath of white flowers. Richard's eyes stung as he read the dedication inscribed beneath an embossed crown and the red, blue and gold heraldic crest of his family. Here in this obscure corner of England the people had kept faith with him. Coming up behind him Gilbert observed drily, "Not quite as universally reviled as you thought, eh, Dickon?" He glanced back at his friend and in that moment the intention behind Gilbert's actions became clearer to him. His mentor seemed to be intent on taking him on a kind of cathartic journey – to the landmarks of his past life, hoping to purge away the negative emotions that held him captive. Richard wondered where they would go next – to Middleham, where he had been happiest? To Barnet and Tewkesbury, where as a youth he had fought beside his brother Edward to regain England's crown? Or even to Ludlow where as a child he was taken prisoner by the Lancastrians along with his mother and brother Clarence?

The shadows of the golden spring afternoon were lengthening when Richard found himself walking towards Leicester. In this city, the monstrous finale of his defeat had played itself out. It was here that the people of England were forcibly made to accept the bloody end of the Plantagenet dynasty, a dynasty that had ruled England for more than three hundred years. Bow Bridge, the ancient boundary to the city, lay ahead. The narrow, arched stone bridge was gone and in its place stood a sturdy, much wider iron structure. On both sides of the bridge crowds of people, many of whom were holding long stemmed white flowers, were being restrained by metal barriers and police in fluorescent yellow jackets. He counted them ten deep as far as the eye could see. An important occasion was in progress. The Mayor, and what looked to be the city's Guild of Freemen in full ceremonial robes and insignia, were assembled at the city end of the bridge, obviously waiting to welcome a VIP. Red and blue banners hung from buildings in the city beyond; they were too far away for him to be able to read their captions but on some he could make out a crown. A royal visitor perhaps? An air of solemn expectation hung over the masses of people lining the pavements. Quiet conversation hummed among the onlookers, a number of whom were engaged in deep and earnest discussion. Suddenly a ripple of excitement ran through the crowds. They surged forward, heads craned, bodies leaning eagerly over the barriers. Sunlight glinting off a shiny police motorbike heralded the arrival at the bridge of a funeral procession. A sleek black hearse, in front of which walked a solemn top-hatted man, began to make its way sedately over the bridge. Richard glimpsed a simple pale oak coffin through its side windows. A length of blue and murrey-coloured cloth was draped over the coffin on which lay a wreath of woodland foliage and white flowers similar to those held by many of the onlookers. Not a day of celebration then but a funeral – and by the look of it, of someone extremely important, thought Richard. He stumbled as a vision of Henry Tudor's triumphant cavalcade crossing over this bridge flashed into his mind. His part in it had been somewhat less than dignified – he had been a bloody corpse slung over the back of a broken-down nag. His mouth twisted at the black humour behind his thoughts; determinedly he pushed the grim image out of his head. The hearse drew to a halt as the mayor led the city fathers out into the road to greet it. He frowned in ever deepening confusion. What possible connection could he have to this event? Swinging round, he searched the monk's face but gained nothing from his expressionless, unreadable features. Snippets of the Mayor's speech drifted towards him in the warm spring air. "…welcoming back…with dignity denied…to honour… rest in peace in Leicester…"

"At least the city did right by him this time," observed a young female nearby.

"Aye, he was a brave man…'twasn't right what that spiteful bugger did to him," observed a gruff male voice. "He had no morals…no honour…"

"And he and his bloodthirsty children and grandchildren then carried out a vendetta against every remaining member of his family that they could get their hands on." Another female joined the conversation, a note of disgust colouring her voice. "Killed them all off one by one…his monster of a son even chopped the head off a poor defenceless old woman…I'll think of her name in a minute…it was very unusual…I remember looking up its meaning when I did some reading after they found him and all these goings on started up…it had something to do with *a pool of water." An uneasy feeling began to crawl up Richard's back. "You are silly, Mum," a child giggled. "Teacher told us all about it in school the other day…it was 'de la Pole'."

Richard was stunned; they were talking about Margaret, his brother Clarence's daughter!

"Shush you lot," admonished a much older man. "They're

moving again; he'll be passing by us any minute now. Get ready to throw your roses."

An inconsequential thought ran through his mind, as he watched an avalanche of white flowers rain down upon the hearse. The flowers were roses; he had not recognized them as such – their tightly packed centres and furling out petals were nothing like the open flat-faced flowers that he had been familiar with when he was alive – but nevertheless they were still the emblem of the house of Plantagenet. He frowned with a sudden shiver of apprehension – who was the person in the coffin that the city of Leicester was 'doing right' by? And who was the 'spiteful bugger' the woman in the crowd had talked about? A small insistent voice in his brain whispered 'Richard III and Henry Tudor'. No! Richard immediately rejected such a notion. This journey into the past was starting to affect his rational thinking. The inferior monument Henry Tudor had commissioned in an attempt to placate England's Yorkists, when faced with Margaret of Burgundy's support of a young man claiming to be Richard of Shrewsbury, younger son of Edward IV, had crumbled away from exposure to the elements, after his son had ordered the destruction of the Greyfriar's monastery. His mortal remains rested lost and forgotten beneath the city. He had no desire for them to be found and for his vile reputation to be resurrected and analysed anew. He had had his fill of the past. It was time to leave. Turning he found his way barred by the monk. The two men stared at each other and in Gilbert's face Richard saw confirmation of what he was trying to deny. Shaking with suppressed anger, he began to speak. "So they found my bones and dug them up," he stated in a hollow voice.

Gilbert said nothing, only gazed back at him with a gleam of determination in his eyes. Getting no response from his friend, Richard's mouth moved in a wintery smile. "And you thought to bring me here today, to see Leicester en fete as they are hauled through the city, an object of curiosity for people to gawp at and comment on!" His jaw tightened momentarily, his fists clenched and unclenched, words of reproach flooded into his brain. Fighting for control he made a violent gesture of denial with one hand. "No more!" he hissed through his teeth. "You will not put me through the shame and humiliation for a second time!"

The monk stepped forward and turned him forcibly to face the hearse. "Fate had not quite finished with you all that time ago, my young friend," he said in a voice made rough with emotion. "Come, we will accompany your mortal remains on their final journey…you will watch and you will listen." Father Gilbert's words made Richard's eyes widen in confusion. His battered corpse had made its final journey centuries ago…hadn't it?

At a walking pace, the hearse wound its way slowly through Leicester's streets. The teeming crowds applauded and threw white roses as it passed; voices cried out 'God save good King Richard!'. Richard's stomach clenched when he heard the words that were last called out to him on his way to do battle for his kingdom. Outside St Nicholas's church, where the cortege paused for a short service of blessing, the waiting onlookers became electrified with anticipation as the sound of the motorcycle was heard once again. Behind it flanked by two mounted police officers and followed by two knights herald in armour that was blindingly bright in the sunshine, was a gun carriage, dark and gleaming, drawn by four coal-black horses. A collective reverential sigh went through the crowds as they watched the pallbearers carefully place the casket upon it.

Richard felt the world begin to spin; Gilbert's grip on his arm steadied him. "Look around, Dickon...here there is no debasement...only respectful crowds with a sense of pride in you. People no longer blindly accept the image of the evil child-murdering king passed down to them through the ages."

Richard's body trembled. He realized that he had read Gilbert's intentions wrongly. This was not a retracing of his past life; he was to be witness to his own reburial. Did he have the strength to go through with this? He bowed his head, silently grappling with his emotions, and the memory of all the horror in the aftermath of his defeat. Finally, he raised his eyes, they locked on to the monk's face, and seeing confirmation written on his craggy features, Richard gathered his resolve. "Then as always, I will put my trust in you, Gilbert," he affirmed thickly.

With a satisfied nod his mentor guided Richard purposefully towards the gun carriage. His long strides slowed and he came to a halt beside it. The monk gazed intently down at the coffin, after a moment he raised assessing eyes to Richard's face. "For countless decades you have studiously ignored anything to do with your life and the time in which you lived..."

Richard gave a short exasperated snort. "For pity's sake, Gilbert, why would I torment myself in such a way? There was never anything that was good, written or said..."

Father Gilbert's raised eyebrows stopped him in mid-sentence. "Listen to me for a moment, Dickon!" he commanded forcefully and then he began to describe how Richard's remains had been treated since their discovery. "Your bones were carefully released from the earth and placed in a box around which was wrapped your royal banner. They were taken to the laboratories of Leicester University and treated with the utmost dignity and care whilst undergoing scientific analysis to ascertain whether they were indeed your mortal remains. Once this was done, they were respectfully coffined and given into the care of the Church. The casket which now contains your bones is lead lined and made of English oak. They lie on a base of unbleached linen, surrounded by soft woollen fleece and covered by thick wool wadding. A rosary blessed by Dominican monks lies on top. An overlay has been tucked around the whole, embroidered with your white boar badges, roses for the house of Plantagenet, and consecration crosses because you were an anointed king." The monk paused and manoeuvred his thoughts for a moment. "It is as if they are making amends; trying to reverse the great wrong done to you in the past." His lips curled in sudden humour. "It could be seen as a 21st century rebuke to Henry Tudor." Hearing his quiet laughter, the heaviness in Richard's chest lifted a little and a tiny kernel of hope began to grow in him.

And right the wrongs of the past the people of present day England most assuredly did. Richard gazed down at the slab of polished Swaledale stone, with its deep cut cross beneath which his remains now lay, and let his mind wander back over the past few days. In a gathering dusk, to the tolling of bells all over the city, an honour guard, wearing red sashes over their khaki uniforms and rows of glinting medals attesting to their service in the country's recent wars, carried his remains into the cathedral. Surprise had stopped him short when they approached it. The

Merchant and Guild church of St Martin had been transformed. It was much larger than he remembered and there was now a tall spire on its old Norman Tower but he could still see traces of the ancient church that he liked to hear Mass in whenever he came to Leicester. They followed the casket over the threshold and found themselves in an English woodland grove of willow, catkins and primroses. White roses decorated every window and although he couldn't see it, the scent of 'planta genista', the sweet broom that was the emblem of his family, hung in the air.

"The men who carry your remains on their shoulders are from regiments that trace their origins back to the shire and city levies that fought for you in the battle," explained Father Gilbert. As an afterthought he added "... known now as the battle of Bosworth Field."

Richard's throat tightened when he saw a Cardinal waiting to meet the coffin as well as the Archbishop of Canterbury. Those who had planned this reburial had remembered that he had died a faithful son of the Catholic Church, before Henry Tudor's son had disavowed the Pope and caused the great rift between England and Rome. He watched as they carried his bones slowly down the nave, past pews packed with royalty, peers of the realm and the nation's military and academic elite. He became conscious of a feeling of great sadness and of a sense of injustice spreading through the congregation. A number of men and women were swallowing hard; others seemed to be blinking back tears. Were they grieving for him – a man who had met his death more than five centuries ago? Richard turned a nonplussed face towards the monk, to see his mentor also deeply affected.

With eyes made bright by a sheen of tears, Father Gilbert

gruffly stated, "You have no knowledge of the sea change that has taken place in the world's attitude to and judgement of you, Dickon. Over many decades historians have studied you more and more closely. They uncovered a loyal, brave, pious and just king. The perception of you as a monstrous Machiavellian tyrant has gone. The evil myth of the 'poisonous bunch-back'd… bloody, and usurping boar' created by William Shakespeare, that brilliant exponent of the Tudors' malign propaganda, is no longer believed. People talk of you with pride as England's last medieval warrior king."

"And also the murderer of my nephews," Richard fired back with dry scepticism.

"Not anymore!" Father Gilbert retorted with swift emphasis. "I cannot deny that there are those who still argue that you killed them but there is now a very real awareness that others stood to gain far more from their deaths than you." Seeing the look of surprise in Richard's face, the monk lapsed into silence and allowed his words to sink in, then continued. "You are also unaware of the enormous worldwide following that you have, Richard. People have travelled far and wide…from all over the world to witness your reburial and to acclaim the warrior king who loved his people and who fought bravely on to the very end. Today, Dickon, you have stepped out from the pages of history and become a very real man to them."

Richard's brain raced as he tried to assimilate all that Gilbert had told him. Suddenly the tiny seed of hope that the monk had planted earlier grew into a full-blown flower.

They set his remains down on a bier in front of the high altar to the beginning of the ancient sunset service of Compline.

A sumptuous, beautifully embroidered black velvet pall was draped over his coffin, on top of which was placed an open gold crown set with enamelled white roses, pearls and what looked to be rubies and sapphires. Richard was struck by its similarity to the circlet he had worn around the helmet of his armour. Beside him Gilbert murmured, "For certain this is meant to symbolise the regaining in death of the crown taken from you in battle."

He got no response from his protégé. Richard's attention was entirely focused on the Book of Hours that had just been placed on a small table at the foot of the casket. It was his own treasured prayer book, the one that he was never parted from. His fingers tingled with an intense desire to hold it once again. Involuntarily his hand reached out, but shaking his head sadly he dropped it to his side – it was an impossibility, he knew. The monk watched him with sympathy, there was no need for Richard to know that it was found in his tent after the battle and given to his nemesis Margaret Stanley.

Richard's eyes were drawn to the four men who had stepped out of the congregation to drape the funeral cloth over his coffin. A sharp stab of pain shot through him when he recognized Thomas Stanley's face amongst them. The traitor had thrived and passed his high forehead and long sharp nose down through the generations of his family. An old bitterness rose up in him, but he forced his eyes away and looked out over the congregation and there he found the familiar features of his cousin and trusted friend, John Howard, Duke of Norfolk, whose loyalty never wavered, who had fought so valiantly and had died beneath the Dadlington windmill on the plain of Redemere. He understood then that bitterness had no place here, only reconciliation.

The hauntingly beautiful service that had meshed together both ancient and modern rites made Richard's heart ache. The poignant recitation of a Collect that long ago he had asked the Middleham priests to repeat daily after his death, and prayers he recalled from his own father's reburial service, had him biting down hard on his lip to retain his composure. The Cardinal's sermon spoke of his being a 'child of war', one who had known little peace in his short life, but he also described Richard as a man of prayer and devotion. Other speakers talked of him being a strong and capable leader, held in high regard by many of those whom he governed; of his being widely read, intelligent, and reflective, with a fierce loyalty to his brother Edward IV. A man of courage who knew the pain of bereavement and loss but yet continued to function, govern and lead. Richard's brain reeled; the image they painted of him was so vastly different from what he had for so long believed it to be. It was unbiased and balanced, there was recognition that he had not always been great and good; that he was a sinner like all the rest of humanity. He was spoken of as a man of his time with whom many people in their modern world could identify. By the time the service came to an end the doubts and misgivings that Richard had harboured, in spite of the monk's assurances, were finally banished. He understood at last the reason behind his return; he had been brought here so that he could see and be part of his renaissance. His heart swelled in gratitude. The burden of guilt and shame that had weighed him down for so long was lifted from his soul; he was finally free.

For three days his remains lay in repose amid the monuments honouring the nation's military dead. Silent veteran warriors stood at each corner of the bier with bowed heads, guarding him night and day whilst people queued for hours to file past and pay their respects. Finally, the honour guard lowered his remains into a brick-lined vault below the floor of the cathedral in a place of honour adjacent to the high altar. It was sealed by a dark marble plinth carved with Richard's name, his coat of arms and his motto 'Loyaulte me lie' on top of which a block of golden Swaledale stone rested. In the silent and empty cathedral Father Gilbert watched Richard carefully, just as he had watched him in the church in the Newarke half a millennium ago when his naked corpse had been displayed on a filthy trestle. The degradation and dishonour inflicted upon his body had all but broken him then. The monk knew that these last days had also tried his protégé's emotions to the utmost. He had to trust that what he had seen and heard would help him come to the right decision but he found it impossible to read Richard's enigmatic features.

Richard looked down at his tomb. The guilt, humiliation and sense of injustice that had burned in him, keeping him captive in Purgatory for so long were gone – wiped from his soul. All that had transpired since this return to the scene of his defeat and death was in complete contrast to what had happened in the past. In these last days he had been honoured as an anointed king and a fallen warrior and he now knew that the vindictive slander of the Tudors was no longer believed. The people of the modern world had given him what had been denied him at the time of his death and, more importantly, they had given him peace. He would be eternally grateful to them but he knew he did not belong in their world. He had been forged in another time and that time had long since passed. His decision made, Richard turned to his mentor and friend. "It's time to return to Eden, Gilbert," he stated quietly.

Together they walked down the nave towards the open doors. They ventured slowly out into the darkening gardens and were brought up short by the citizens of Leicester's last tribute to him: there, emblazoned in light on the steeple, was a crown with 'RIII' beneath it and on the ground in front of them the tiny flames of thousands of candles flickered and danced in the still evening air. Richard's throat was suddenly constricted, it was difficult to swallow. He found himself struggling to hold back the hot tears burning behind his eyes. Movement in the shadows beneath the cathedral walls caught his attention. He watched as two robed figures stepped out of the lengthening twilight; the larger of the two wore the habit of the Franciscan Order. Silently they walked towards him, coming to a halt a short distance away. The slighter figure stepped forward and raised its head; slim white hands pushed back the hood that hid its face and Richard found himself gazing into the soft grey eyes of Anne Neville, his beloved wife.

~ ~ ~ ~ ~

Notes

I hope any Medieval Historians and Richard III purists who read this story will forgive me for allowing him a moment of victory – for him to break through the pike barrier and have Henry at his mercy before disaster overtakes him.

There is much conjecture about the relationship between Richard and Anne Neville. Given the fact that Richard rescued her from the kitchen/cook-shop in which his brother the Duke of Clarence had hidden her and placed her in sanctuary; that he renounced most of her father Richard Neville's land and property including the Earldoms of Warwick and Salisbury, and surrendered to Clarence the office of Great Chamberlain of England in order to marry her; and as the brother of the king of England he could have had his pick of eligible noblewomen or foreign princesses but instead chose the impoverished daughter of a traitor and widow of the heir of the opposing faction, I have chosen to portray them as childhood sweethearts and their marriage to have been a love match.

*William Colyngbourne had close ties to the Woodvilles. He was High Sherriff of Wiltshire, Somerset and Dorset, and Commissioner of the Peace. He set up the charges of Treason against George Duke of Clarence. He gained property in Wiltshire after Clarence's execution. Deprived of the power he enjoyed under the Woodvilles, in July 1483 he paid Thomas Yate to contact Henry Tudor and Thomas Grey Marquess of Dorset to urge them to invade in October and contacted French Court with a false warning of Richard's intention to invade France. The rhyme was pinned on the door of St Paul's in July 1484. He was tried for high treason, not for the rhyme as is popularly believed. To fit my story I have moved the release of the rhyme forward by a few months.

*Many medieval theologians believed that the Garden of Eden was located on earth – made remote and inaccessible by deserts and lofty mountain ranges.

*In 1789 workmen repairing St George's chapel rediscovered and accidentally broke into Edward IV's vault and discovered a smaller adjoining vault containing the coffins of two mysterious unidentified children. No inspection was carried out and the tomb was resealed and inscribed with the names of two children who predeceased Edward, namely: George Duke of Bedford (died aged 2) and Mary of York (died aged 14). During excavations for the royal tomb of George III under the Wolsey tomb in 1810-13, two lead coffins clearly labelled George and Mary were discovered and moved into the vault adjoining Edward IV's. No effort was made to identify the two lead coffins already in the vault. Could they be the lost princes in the Tower? For the purpose of my story I have decided that they are and that their uncle Richard III placed them there.

*In his only Parliament Richard gave the country bail, the presumption of innocence, protection from corrupt jurors and tainted jury verdicts, a right to representation and a statute of limitations.

*The meaning of the surname de la Pole is – of or by the water.

*Reincarnation is commonly represented in the Western world as an exclusively Hindu and Buddhist doctrine but is was a tenet of Orthodox Judaism - 'gilgul or ha'atakah believed the immortal soul went from birth to birth until it attained salvation which ended the cycle of rebirth. In Christ's time it was believed that the soul remained in the earth's astral atmosphere to await rebirth: 'The air is full of souls; those who are nearest to earth descending to be tied to mortal bodies return to other bodies, desiring to live in them.'

Lightning Source UK Ltd.
Milton Keynes UK
UKHW04f0900310718
326552UK00001B/19/P